Look what people are saying about this talented author's latest works.

"Vicki Lewis Thompson gives readers
a sexy, funny tale."
—*Romance Reviews Today* on
Better Naughty than Nice

"Hang on for the ride of your life…
I could not put this book down!"
—*Night Owl Reviews* on *Blonde with a Wand*

"If you thought *Over Hexed* was phenomenal,
wait until you read *Wild & Hexy!*…
A rip-roaring good time."
—*Romance Junkies*

"The same trademark blend of comedy and heart that
won Thompson's Nerd series a loyal following."
—*Publishers Weekly* on *Over Hexed*

"Thompson mixes magic, small-town quirkiness
and passionate sex for a winsome effect."
—*BookList* on *Over Hexed*

CLAIMED!

BY
VICKI LEWIS THOMPSON

To all those compassionate souls who have cared
for a child not their own, and who have never let the
circumstances of birth stop them from doing
what needed to be done.

New York Times bestselling author **Vicki Lewis Thompson** has been writing books for a few (cough, cough) years now, and she has a Nora Roberts Lifetime Achievement Award from Romance Writers of America to prove it. Turns out that after all these years and all these books, the process is as exciting and challenging as ever. In other words, the one hundred and first book is no easier to write than the first! And she wouldn't have it any other way. This is a great job and somebody has to do it. She feels lucky that she's been allowed to share her fantasy world with readers everywhere.

Dear Reader,

Summer nights are cool in Wyoming, but the right cowboy can raise the temperature in no time! And I have just the cowboy for you. Join me while we follow Jack, the oldest Chance brother, as he calls on his ex-girlfriend, Josie, owner of the Spirits and Spurs Saloon.

The bar is closed and Shoshone's Main Street is deserted. If you listen carefully, you'll hear the hoot of an owl perched on a nearby lamppost. The moon peeks out from a passing cloud, but Jack doesn't need its light to find his way. It's been ten long months since he climbed the stairs to Josie's apartment above the bar, but he could do it blindfolded.

Many things have changed, though, in those ten months. Jack's now in charge of running the Last Chance Ranch, a place dedicated to those who deserve a last chance at happiness. And if anyone needs that, it's the broad-shouldered cowboy climbing those wooden stairs. Come listen to Jack's story. And welcome back!

Warmly,

Vicki

Prologue

"BEAR DOWN, Eleanor!" Delia, a midwife from Jackson, coached the birth from the foot of Archie and Nelsie Chance's marriage bed. "This little tyke's a stubborn one."

Archie gripped his wife's hand. "Not as stubborn as my wife," he said with pride. He'd watched her battle for five hours to have this baby. Her language had grown more colorful, but her spirit had never flagged. He crouched down and murmured in her ear. "Come on, Nelsie girl. You can do it."

Nelsie panted and dug her nails into his hand. "Damn right I can. This kid is going to be born…right…*now!*" And she let out a yell that would have done a cowhand proud.

Delia whooped. "That does it!" She eased the baby free. "Congratulations. You have yourselves a bouncing baby boy."

Still clutching Nelsie's hand, Archie rose to his feet

and stared in wonder. The baby was as red as a boiled lobster and slippery with goo. As Delia ran a cloth over the wrinkled little face, the baby sputtered once before launching into a series of high-pitched, hiccuping wails. Archie's vision blurred and his chest tightened. A son. He had a son.

"Archie?" Nelsie squeezed his hand. "Are you okay?"

Clearing his throat, he blinked away tears. "I've never been more okay in my life." He leaned down to give her a tender kiss. "How about you, brave girl?"

"Much better, now."

"Thank you for having our baby."

Nelsie looked a little misty-eyed herself. "My pleasure. Well, maybe not. It was a lot more fun making that baby than having him."

"I'll bet." He kissed her again. "You were great."

"So who wants to hold him first?" Delia approached with the squalling baby wrapped in a blanket.

Archie had assisted many a calf into this life and a few foals, as well, but holding this baby scared the bejesus out of him. "Maybe you'd better give him to Nelsie."

"No." Nelsie's voice was firm. "You hold him first, Arch. I want Delia to take a picture. The camera's on the dresser."

"Uh, okay." Archie could hardly refuse after all Nelsie had been through. Reluctantly he accepted the red-faced little kid, who was working up quite a head of steam. "Just for the picture."

"Support his head in the crook of your arm." Delia

positioned the baby to her satisfaction. "There. I'll get the camera. By the way, have you picked a name?"

Archie stood frozen to the spot and gazed down at the tiny face, the eyes squeezed shut and the toothless mouth pouring out all that baby anguish.

"We decided on Jonathan Edward," he said. "Jonathan for Nelsie's father and Edward for mine."

"That's a fine name," Delia said. "Suits him."

Archie wasn't sure. It seemed like a really big name for such a tiny thing. "Shh," he murmured, jiggling the baby just a little bit, the way he'd seen people do. "Shh, Jonathan."

As if a switch had been thrown, the baby stopped crying. With a ragged sigh, Jonathan Edward opened his little eyes.

"See?" Nelsie's voice trembled. "He likes his name."

"Guess so." Archie's chest swelled as he looked into those unfocused baby eyes.

"Hold still so I can get the picture," Delia said.

Archie didn't glance up as the camera flashed. That newborn gaze held all his attention. Slowly he began to contemplate something he hadn't dared think about until now. Life held no guarantees, but with a little luck, this tiny baby would grow into his name. And with even more luck, Jonathan Edward Chance would continue the legacy of the Last Chance Ranch.

1

Present day

"Josie, there's a drunken cowboy at the door."

Jack Chance stared at the tall guy silhouetted in the doorway of Josie's place. *His* Josie. "Who the hell are you?"

"That's none of your business. Look, Josie closed the bar thirty minutes ago, and besides, you don't look as if you need another—"

"You'd better not be her boyfriend." Jack was a tad bit liquored up, but he'd been sober enough to climb the stairs to Josie's apartment above the Spirits and Spurs without stumbling. He also was sober enough to understand the significance of a guy answering her door at this hour of the night.

The intruder shifted his stance. "And you'd better be on your way, cowboy."

That's when Jack noticed the bastard wasn't wearing shoes or socks. Jack's blood boiled. How dare this yahoo move in on *his* girl? True, they'd broken up a few months ago. Okay, ten months ago. But just who did this idiot think he was, standing barefoot in Josie's apartment like he owned the place?

"Alex?" Josie's voice came from somewhere in the back of the apartment. *Like the bedroom.* "Find out who it is, okay?"

Jack clenched his right fist. "The name's Jonathan Edward Chance, Jr., and Josie Keller's my girl." Then he punched this Alex joker smack in the kisser.

Sad to say, it wasn't much of a blow. Jack wasn't as steady as he might have been and the guy dodged at the last minute. Failing to land a solid punch, Jack dropped his shoulder and threw a tackle. That proved to be more effective. They both went down hard. Jack lost his hat and a good part of his dignity.

Alex swore and struggled to get free, but Jack had him pinned. It was a hollow victory, though, because Jack had knocked the wind clean out of himself.

"What in the name of heaven is going on?"

I'm guarding my territory. The thought went through Jack's head, but he didn't have the breath to say it.

"Jack Chance, get off my brother this minute!"

Thank God he hadn't said it. Her brother? Jee-sus. The back of his neck grew hot as he pushed himself to his hands and knees.

Alex glared up at him. He didn't look happy. But he did look quite a bit like Josie. Same blond hair, same gray eyes. Come to think of it, Josie had mentioned an older brother named Alex, but he was supposed to be in Chicago, not standing in her doorway barefoot, giving the wrong impression that he was fixing to be Jack's replacement.

"Sorry about that, man." Jack staggered to his feet and held out a hand to help the guy up.

Alex ignored Jack's outstretched hand and stood under his own power. Then he turned to Josie. "I take it you know this jerk."

Josie must have been getting ready for bed. She was wearing that silky black robe Jack remembered, but her jeans peeked out underneath, so she hadn't completed undressing when Jack had arrived. She hadn't taken her long hair out of its braid, either. Jack used to love when she did that. He used to love everything Josie did.

She sighed. "Yes, I know him. This is Jack Chance, the guy I was dating last year."

Dating. Such a lame word for what they'd had going. Josie made it sound as if they'd kept each other company during the occasional dinner, followed by a PG-rated movie. Instead they'd spent hours having wild monkey sex in this apartment. Sometimes they'd even used the bed. There wasn't a piece of furniture in the place that didn't remind Jack of being buck naked with Josie.

Well, maybe the stove. They'd never done it on the stove, because sure as the world they would have hit a switch in the midst of the crazy action and singed something vital. They couldn't get enough of each other back then.

Alex's eyes narrowed and he clenched his fists at his sides. "So this is the one."

Stepping neatly between Jack and Alex, Josie put a

hand on her brother's chest. "I'm not angry about that anymore, Alex."

Jack got a whiff of her perfume, which had always reminded him of peach schnapps. God, how he'd missed her.

"You may not be angry anymore, but I'm pissed as hell." Alex's jaw tightened. "As I recall, this SOB dropped you like a hot potato when his dad died. And now he has the unmitigated gall to barge in here as if—"

"I thought you were her new boyfriend, Keller. Sorry." Nobody had ever accused Jack of having unmitigated gall. Not many folks around Shoshone, Wyoming, talked that way. He'd been accused of having a hell of a lot of nerve, but never unmitigated gall.

Last Jack had heard, Alex was a DJ for one of Chicago's drive-time radio shows. Stood to reason he'd have a big-deal vocabulary to go with his job.

"And what if I had been her boyfriend, hotshot?" Alex balanced on the balls of his feet. "You think you can dictate who she sees? Somebody needs to teach you some manners."

Jack figured the guy could start swinging any minute. Although Jack had never had a sister, he could imagine how a brother might feel toward someone who had treated his sister the way Jack had treated Josie. He wasn't proud of his actions, but at the time they'd made some sort of crazy sense.

He'd been in bed with Josie the morning his dad had called wanting his help to pick up a filly from a nearby ranch. Jack had put him off with the excuse that a storm was brewing, when actually he hadn't wanted to leave Josie. His dad had gone alone, rolled the truck and died. Riddled with guilt, Jack had punished himself the only way he knew how. He'd told Josie they were finished.

No wonder Alex wanted to punch his lights out. Any brother worth his salt would feel the same. Jack had never been one to back down from a fight if he believed in the cause, but this time he was in the wrong and he knew it.

"I'll just leave, then," he said.

Josie relaxed a little. "Good idea, Jack."

He started for the door and paused to glance over his shoulder. "I really did think he was your new boyfriend."

She gazed at him with eyes the color of a storm cloud. "And that would bother you?"

His brain definitely wasn't working, because he hadn't realized until that moment how his caveman tactics had exposed him. "Reflex," he said, trying to pawn the punch off as nothing more than habit.

"I see."

"Pure knee-jerk reaction. See you all later." It might have been a decent exit if he hadn't tripped on the door-sill. He didn't fall, but he came damned close to it. Face burning, he started down the wooden stairway to the street level. If Josie told anybody about this, he'd never hear the end of it.

"Jack, wait." Josie caught up with him partway down and laid a hand on his arm. "You shouldn't drive home."

He glanced back at her. Her hair had come a little bit

loose from her braid, and the porch light shone on the top of her head, creating a kind of halo. He knew for a fact she was no angel, but damn, she was beautiful.

"I'm okay," he said. "Just clumsy." He wasn't about to tell her he had no vehicle at his disposal. He hadn't intended to come into town at all tonight.

He'd been at the ranch quietly getting soused. It was his pathetic attempt to ease the crushing sense of responsibility he felt now that he was in charge of everything. He'd been interrupted in that endeavor when his youngest brother, Gabe, had come home devastated because Morgan, the woman he loved, had turned down his marriage proposal.

Jack had convinced him to drive back into town and repeat the proposal with Jack riding shotgun and giving moral support.

"Leave your truck here and let me drive you home," Josie said.

"Sorry. Too humiliating."

"Don't be stupid, Jack. Your family doesn't need another tragedy."

A reminder like that still had the power to slice through him. "That's a cheap shot."

"Maybe, but I don't want to find out tomorrow that you drove into a tree on the way home, so I'm willing to fight dirty. Your truck will be fine here." She glanced down at the parking area. "Where *is* your truck, by the way? I don't see it."

Jack sighed. Gabe would pay for this. When Gabe's second proposal had worked out, Gabe had disappeared inside Morgan's house, taking the truck keys with him.

On his way in, he'd suggested Jack go knock on Josie's door. Lured by his brother's success with his woman, Jack had decided to go for broke.

Which had landed him in this pile of stinking cow manure.

"Josie, just go back inside and let me take care of my own problems, okay?"

She crossed her arms over her chest. "No."

"What do you mean, *no?* Are you planning to sling me over your shoulder and throw me in the back of your Bronco?"

"I mean that you owe me, Jack Chance. You owe me big time for the way you acted ten months ago. I don't want things to get any uglier because you drove away from my place and got in a wreck. Your family already blames me for—"

"They don't."

"Not to my face, but it was because of me you didn't pick up that filly with your dad. If I hadn't been in the picture, he might still be alive."

"Good God, is that what you think? That it's somehow your fault?" Jack was stunned. He thought he had the corner on guilt, but maybe not.

"Logically I know it wasn't my fault. You're a big boy."

"My point exactly. About that morning and tonight. Go back inside. I'm not your problem."

She didn't budge. "Logically I get that. But emotionally...that's a whole other thing. I wish I'd kicked you out of bed that morning, Jack. I wish I'd told you to go help your dad trailer that filly to the Last Chance."

"Wasn't your call."

"So *you* don't blame me?"

He heard the pain in her voice and knew that he'd caused it. "I never did."

"Then why'd you end…us?"

"Some sort of penance, I guess. Thought I didn't deserve to be happy." And he had been happy. *They* had been happy. In his slightly inebriated state tonight, he'd deluded himself into thinking that the problems between them would magically evaporate and they could be happy again.

She bowed her head for a moment. When she looked at him, her gaze was direct. "I'm driving you home. Stay right here while I put my shirt on and get my wallet and keys."

"Josie, I can—"

"Do it, Jack! Let's stop the bullshit and do the sensible thing for once! I didn't kick you out of bed ten months ago, but I damned sure won't let you drive home tonight. I won't have it on my conscience."

She was fired up, and he couldn't say he blamed her. After all, he was the one who had knocked on her door. Gabe had suggested it, but he hadn't twisted Jack's arm. Once again, Jack knew who was to blame for this disaster. "All right," he said. "I'll wait here until you get back."

"LET ME drive him home," Alex said once Josie announced her intentions. "You shouldn't be dealing with that jerk."

"I appreciate your protectiveness, but better me

than you." Josie smiled at him. She loved having her only sibling around, although she hated his reason for coming.

His divorce from Crystal had become final this week, and he'd taken unused vacation time to get some perspective on the situation. Crystal had initiated the proceedings, and he still hadn't recovered from the shock.

Only two years apart, Josie and Alex had fought like wildcats as kids, but as adults they were the best of friends. Alex was the first person Josie called for advice, and vice-versa. They were always there for each other, and she was happy to have him camp out on her hide-a-bed for as long as he needed to.

"What if I promise not to rough him up?" Alex said.

Josie laughed as she headed into the bedroom to change out of her bathrobe. "I wouldn't believe you. You should have seen yourself once you knew who he was. You all but pawed the ground."

Alex followed her down the short hallway of her apartment. "Have you forgotten how miserable you were when he pulled the plug on the relationship?"

"No, I haven't forgotten." She turned and looked at her blond Adonis of a brother. Crystal was an idiot who'd never appreciated him. "Tell me this, Alex. If you thought there was a chance to start over with Crystal, would you take it?"

He hesitated. "I don't know. We've said some things that can't be unsaid."

"Same with me and Jack. But we meant a lot to each

other once." More than a lot. Jack had been everything to her, and she'd kidded herself that he felt the same. Then he'd spoken those horrible words that she'd never forget—*No big deal, Josie. It was just sex.*

"Be careful, sis."

"I will." And she would be, she vowed as she went into her bedroom to exchange her robe for the western shirt she'd thrown on the bed. Ten months ago, when she'd been more gullible, Jack had been capable of cutting her off at the knees.

But since then she'd admitted to herself that she'd woven a fantasy out of nothing. Jack had never told her he loved her, never suggested they could spend their lives together. No matter what happened between her and Jack now, she wouldn't wear rose-colored glasses ever again.

She liked having the advantage that he'd come to her, though. True, he was slightly drunk and his guard was down. Ever since the painful phone call announcing Jonathan's death and the end of their relationship, Jack had avoided the Spirits and Spurs. Josie had run into him a few times in town, and he'd remained polite but distant. He wasn't that way now, but he could be again.

In fact, she could count on it. Jack didn't like to be vulnerable, and that's exactly what he'd been tonight. He didn't want her driving him home, but she'd played her trump card by reminding him that his dad had been killed behind the wheel.

She'd played that card willingly. Jack might be able to navigate the rural two-lane between Shoshone and the Last Chance Ranch, but she wasn't going to risk it. If anything happened to him…

Grabbing her wallet, her cell phone and the keys to her Bronco, she headed down the hall.

Alex stood and tossed aside the magazine he'd been reading. "I'm going. Mom and Dad told me to keep an eye on you while I was out here, and this qualifies."

"You're not going."

"I don't trust him."

"I'm perfectly safe, Alex. Jack may have broken my heart, but he'd never harm me. Underneath all that bluster is a very gentle soul."

Alex snorted. "So I noticed when he assaulted me."

"That was a mistake."

"Oh, it was a mistake, all right. Now he's on my list."

"Please don't judge him by tonight. He's not that kind of guy."

"What kind of guy is he?"

"Confused. His mom left when he was three. He pretends it was no big deal, but I think it colors everything."

Alex gazed at her. "You're still in love with him."

Josie opened her mouth to protest, but she knew it would be a lie. She'd tried to stop loving Jack, but she hadn't had much luck. She'd meshed with him in a way she hadn't with any other man. Their conversation came easily and their silences were never uncomfortable.

Then there was the sexual connection. His deep voice still haunted her dreams. She'd wake in the middle of the night, hot and aching for his touch.

With Jack she'd lost all her inhibitions. She'd felt alive, sensual, beautiful. Several people had warned her that he was a playboy who never stayed with a woman for long.

Some said it all went back to his mother leaving. Jack didn't want to be left again, they figured, so he made sure he cut out before another woman could hurt him. But his affair with Josie had lasted six glorious months and he'd shown no signs of leaving.

Extraordinary circumstances had ended the relationship. Josie wondered what would have happened if Jonathan Chance hadn't died and reawakened all Jack's fears of being abandoned by those he loved. It was clear Jack hadn't forgotten about her if he'd come here tonight ready to fight for her.

Alex sighed. "So you're in love with him. Unfortunately, I don't think that he's—"

"Maybe he isn't in love with me, but we were building something together. Then when his dad died, it all went to hell."

"He was cruel and insensitive. Those are your words, by the way, not mine."

"I know, but people can change. They can escape their past."

"Oh, Josie, don't fall into that trap." Then he laughed and scrubbed a hand over his face. "Listen to me, giving you advice when my love life is in the dumper."

Josie moved closer and gave him a hug. "I'll be okay. Don't worry about me."

"Too late. I'm already worried. Listen, tell that guy that if he doesn't treat you like royalty, he'll answer to me. He doesn't want to mess with somebody who grew up on the mean streets of Chi-town."

"You did not. You grew up in Arlington Heights."

He grinned. "Yeah, but that doesn't mean I don't have connections. I know people who know people. Mention cement overshoes to him."

She stood on tiptoe and kissed him on the cheek. "I'll do that." As if it would matter, but she didn't say that to Alex. Jack Chance had been through hell and back. He wasn't afraid of anyone or anything.

2

JACK CHOSE TO WAIT for Josie beside her dark green Bronco. As he leaned against the fender, cool night air blew most of the cobwebs from his brain and left him with a clear and present truth. He'd behaved like an ass tonight.

He'd been doing that quite a bit lately, but tonight could qualify as his most spectacular display of assholeness in his entire thirty-two years. If they gave out medals for being a complete loser, he would win the gold, hands down.

As his punishment, he would accept this ride home from Josie, because the reality was, he didn't have a lot of choice. Rousting Gabe out of Morgan's bed and demanding the keys to his truck would only add to Jack's list of transgressions. Sure, he could walk home, but that would take a good hour, maybe closer to two. And besides, everyone knew cowboys didn't walk.

So instead he waited for Josie and stared up at the unlit sign of a cowboy on a bucking bronco, with Spirits

and Spurs lettered underneath. The bar used to be called
The Rusty Spur, but Josie had changed the name when
she'd bought the place three years ago. Newcomers to
Shoshone assumed the Spirits part referred to alcohol.
A person had to stick around a while to find out that
Josie considered the bar haunted. Many locals played
along and called the after-hours visitors Ghost Drinkers
in the Bar.

Jack didn't believe in ghosts. More specifically, he
didn't *want* to believe in ghosts. All he needed was to
have his father come back from the dead and tell him
he was screwing up the management of the ranch.

He probably was. Everyone complained that he
worked them too hard, that he worked himself too hard.
But he was in charge of the whole operation now, and
he'd be damned if the Last Chance would go in the red
on his watch.

He'd never wanted to be in charge, but his dad had
assumed he would be someday. Jack hadn't known
how to tell him that he didn't want that honor, that he'd
rather have Nick or Gabe run the place. It had seemed
ungrateful.

His unspoken dream was to take over as foreman
when Emmett retired. He'd intended to propose that to
Jonathan eventually, but he'd procrastinated and now it
was too late. He would do what was expected of him.

Footsteps on gravel alerted him that Josie had arrived.
He turned to watch her walk in his direction. Even in
the dim light from the dusk-to-dawn lamp he could tell
her expression was wary.

He ached for a return to the old days, when she'd

greeted him with a smile brighter than a summer morning. Those days were gone, and if he'd had any idea of recapturing them, he'd ruined that possibility by attacking her brother and making a fool of himself in the process.

"An apology seems pretty lame under the circumstances," he said. "But I'm offering one, anyway. I'm sorry I tried to punch out your brother."

Her wary expression changed and she began to laugh. "*Tried* being the operative word. I've never seen you so uncoordinated, Jack."

Her laughter helped ease the tension. "Good thing I wasn't at my best, then. You'd be a lot more pissed at me if I'd rearranged his face."

"He also would have rearranged yours. He might be a city boy, but he's no slouch when it comes to a fight."

Jack admired her loyal streak. Ten months ago, he'd been entitled to that loyalty, too. "I don't doubt it. He's your brother."

That seemed to sit well with her, and she smiled. "And he's more protective than I remembered. He told me to mention the possibility of cement overshoes."

"In Wyoming?"

She shrugged.

"He needs to acclimate to the western way of doing things. Out here we bury people up to their necks in ant hills and pour honey on them."

"Duly noted." She pulled her keys out of her jeans pocket. "Ready to go?"

"Sure." He would rather stand out here and talk until

dawn the way they had the first time they'd recognized their mutual attraction.

He'd never forget that spring night. He'd flirted with her at the bar and then stayed until closing. She'd walked him out to the parking lot and they'd talked until sunup. Before he'd driven away, he'd kissed her and promised that the next night they'd do more than talk. And boy howdy, had they. They'd burned up the sheets that first night, and many nights afterward.

As he climbed into her Bronco, he realized he'd never been a passenger in her vehicle. They'd gone into Jackson a few times during the six months they'd been lovers, but he'd always driven. This reversal of roles felt weird. It threw him off his game.

When she got in, bringing with her the scent of peach schnapps, he braced himself for the tough part—being this close without touching her. They used to ride down the road with their hands entwined. A few times they'd parked somewhere secluded and made out because they couldn't wait for the privacy of her apartment.

"Buckle up, cowboy."

"Right." He'd been caught staring at her and reminiscing. Not cool. He latched his seat belt and took a deep breath. "Thanks for driving me home."

"No problem." She started the engine. "Just where is your truck, anyway? I seriously doubt you walked into town."

"I rode in with Gabe. We…had an errand over at Morgan's."

"Oh?" She pulled the Bronco onto the two-lane

main road, which was deserted at this hour. "So where's Gabe?"

"Still at Morgan's, I'm sure."

"Oh." She caught the green at Shoshone's only stoplight and headed toward the edge of town. "So they're back together?"

"Looks like." Jack thought it was Gabe and Morgan's business when they announced the engagement. Although the ending to the evening could stand improvement in his case, he was happy that those two had patched things up.

"I'm beginning to get the picture." Josie increased the Bronco's speed as they left the town limits. "You had nowhere else to go, so you came over to my place."

"You make it sound like a last resort."

"Wasn't it?"

"No. I could have…" She had him there. He had some buddies in town, but he'd made himself scarce recently because of the ranch responsibilities. After blowing his friends off every time they'd asked him to meet them for a beer, he couldn't very well show up in the middle of the night looking for a ride home or a place on the couch.

"Reliable old Josie." Her good humor seemed to have faded some. "A guy can always count on her to take him in, right?"

"That's not the way I was thinking." Fact was, he hadn't been thinking or he would have figured out an alternative. Worse came to worse, he could have gone to Grandma Judy's. Technically she wasn't his grandmother. She was his stepmother, Sarah's, mom.

She would have taken him in, though. And then told Sarah all about it the next day. He could have weathered that, but he wasn't about to get an eighty-six-year-old woman out of bed, especially one who'd had a hip replacement barely two months ago.

"To think I imagined you'd chosen to come over to my place," Josie said. "Instead I was just handy."

"You have it all wrong!" The more she voiced the truth, the harder he'd deny it.

"No I don't. Man up and admit it, Jack. I was the alternative to sleeping on a park bench, nothing more."

"Is this why you offered to drive me home? So you could chew my ass all the way there?" Not that he blamed her.

"I offered because I'm a bartender, and I'm trained to recognize when someone is impaired and shouldn't drive. I thought you had your truck and were about to get in it. I didn't know you were stranded."

"So if you'd known I didn't have a truck to drive, you would have let me walk?"

She didn't answer.

"You would have, wouldn't you? Well, we can take care of that right now. Pull over."

"No."

"Pull over, damn it!"

"I said I'd drive you home and I will drive you home. I honor my commitments."

"What do you mean by that crack?"

Her jaw tightened. "I think you know."

She'd pushed him too far. Jack Chance always honored his word. "We didn't have a *commitment*."

"Oh, good one, Jack! No woman ties you down, does she? You can spend every spare minute getting naked with her, but I guess it's all about the sex, just like you said that day, because when it comes to making a *commitment,* you just can't see yourself doing that, can you?" Her voice sounded funny, sort of choked up.

He peered at her in the dim light of the dashboard. "Josie, are you crying?"

"No!" She swiped at her cheeks. "Got something in my eye."

He didn't buy it. She was crying, and that rattled him. In six months of being together, he'd never seen her cry. Of course, he'd broken up with her over the phone, because he couldn't have done it in person. In person, he wouldn't have been able to say the one thing that he knew would convince her they were finished—*it was just sex.* After delivering that message, he'd hung up quickly. He'd probably made her cry then, but he'd avoided thinking about that.

"Josie."

"That's my name. Don't wear it out."

He sighed. "I'm sorry for…everything." He doubted a global apology would do much good, but he wasn't experienced at saying he was sorry.

She cleared her throat. "No reason to apologize, Jack. You're just being you. I guess you got tired of the celibate life, huh?"

"*What?*"

"I know you haven't been seeing anybody since we broke up. Everybody says you've become a workaholic. Stands to reason that given a free night in town with no truck available, you'd look up the woman you used to have sex with. Perfectly logical."

"Damn it to hell! That's not why I came to see you tonight!" But it was, in a way. He'd had some vague idea that she might be glad to see him after all this time. She hadn't hooked up with anyone, either, or at least that's what he'd thought until he'd seen a guy standing in her doorway.

"It's okay, Jack."

No, it wasn't. Everything was a gold-plated mess. He'd followed Gabe's suggestion in hopes that he'd be able to make up with Josie and return to an uncomplicated relationship built on laughter and sex. At least he'd always considered the relationship uncomplicated.

Clearly he'd been wrong.

Jack didn't know what to say that would help the situation, and Josie seemed all talked out, so they drove in silence the rest of the way to the ranch. The long road in from the highway was unpaved because that's how Jack's father had wanted it. Jonathan Chance thought an unpaved road would discourage gawkers, while true horsemen and women determined to see the registered Paints bred by the Last Chance wouldn't be deterred by a little dirt and dust.

Jack wasn't about to pave the road and go against tradition, but as Josie's Bronco jolted over the ruts, he vowed to have it graded soon. Maybe he'd rent a grader and do it himself.

At last Josie eased to a stop in the circular gravel drive in front of the two-story ranch house. Constructed of logs by Jack's grandfather Archie, the house had grown as the family expanded. The right wing was added when Jack's father was born, and he'd built the left wing as his three boys grew older and needed more space.

Each wing was angled so that the house seemed to offer an embrace. Or a trap.

"This is a big place," Josie said, breaking the silence.

"Yeah." Jack didn't need to be reminded. Big place. Big responsibility.

"I know I've been out here before, but everything was…different."

"My dad was still alive."

"Right. But tonight, driving through Chance land, and then seeing the house and the outbuildings again… it's made me realize what a huge job you inherited last October." She stared straight ahead, as if fixated on the house. "I remember you said once that you didn't want to be in charge of the Last Chance."

"I can handle it." What else was he supposed to say? He wasn't going to lay his troubles at her feet like some jerk looking for sympathy.

"I'm sure you can." She glanced at him. "Take care of yourself, Jack."

He recognized a kiss-off remark when he heard it. She was done with him. He shouldn't be surprised. After ten months of silence he'd shown up slightly drunk, with no advance warning, and he'd laid into her brother.

Good thing he hadn't counted on her welcoming him back. This had been an experiment, and it had failed spectacularly. With practiced ease, he closed off his heart.

"See you around." It was a phrase he used a lot, but in this case it was inappropriate. He wouldn't be seeing her around, not if he could help it. Not if she could help it, either, he was sure. He got out of the truck and walked toward the darkened house.

Behind him gravel crunched as she drove away. Well, that was over with. Completely over.

As she headed back to Shoshone, Josie refused to let herself cry again. She'd already shed way too many tears over Jack Chance. But she couldn't seem to do anything about the ache in her chest. She'd reopened a wound that had finally started to heal, and now she remembered what that pain had felt like.

When she'd imagined him coming back, and she'd done that far too often for her own good, she'd expected him to make some grand gesture, something worthy of a Chance man. Instead their reunion had been an afterthought, the by-product of whatever had happened with Morgan and Gabe. Man, that hurt.

She reached Shoshone in record time. Fortunately no cops were around to see her put the pedal to the metal and hurtle down that two-lane road away from the Last Chance Ranch, away from Jack Chance and his half-assed apologies. It would be a cold day in hell before she ever gave that guy room in her heart.

This time she'd tamp down any remaining sparks of hope that they could rekindle the flame between them. Jack was a lost cause. She should have realized that a long time ago, but she did now. Whether his issues arose from his mother leaving him when he was a toddler or his father dying in a rollover that Jack felt he could have prevented, the guy obviously wasn't ready to deal with his demons.

She parked next to the Spirits and Spurs and climbed the stairs to her apartment. Although she loved her brother to distraction, she wanted to be alone right now. But she had to let him know she was home or he'd worry about her.

When she walked in, Alex was sitting on the couch reading the same news magazine he'd had earlier. He glanced up immediately. "Well?"

"It's over for good this time." She ignored the way her chest tightened when she said that.

"You don't look happy, but it's probably for the best. In the long run, I mean."

"It is." She took a shaky breath. "I thought he'd put some thought into coming over here. I even told myself he'd been drinking to bolster his courage to face me. But he only dropped by because his brother stranded him in town. He had nowhere else to go."

"Aw, sis." Alex stood and came toward her, as if he wanted to give her a hug.

She held up a hand. "Don't be too sympathetic or I might lose it, and I'm determined not to do that. The bastard doesn't deserve my tears."

"No, he doesn't. But he deserves some grief from me. If you'll point me in the direction of this ranch of his, I'd like to—"

"Thanks, but no thanks, Alex. I appreciate the sentiment. I really do. But you ending up in a physical confrontation with Jack isn't going to help anything. Besides, he's... He's in really good shape."

She'd tried to avoid thinking about that hard body of his the entire time they'd been cooped inside the Bronco together. She'd failed. The minute she'd breathed in his scent, a combination of leather, spice and virile male, she'd experienced total recall of what that body could accomplish with a willing woman.

Had he touched her, she might have forgiven him everything. She was lucky he hadn't tried.

"I'm in good shape, too," Alex said quietly. "And it would give me great satisfaction to cause him some pain after what he's put you through."

She shook her head. "That would only stir the pot. The best way to handle Jack Chance is to ignore him completely. I intend to, and I'd like you to do the same."

"But—"

"Please, Alex."

"Okay." He shrugged. "It's your town."

"Not really. If it's anybody's town, it belongs to the Chance family. They're the reigning royalty around here."

Alex crossed his arms and studied her. "I'll bet there's a quaint little bar for sale somewhere in downtown Chicago."

"I wouldn't give Jack the satisfaction of running me out. I love it here, and the bar's doing very well. At this rate I'll have the building paid for in five years. I'm staying." She lifted her chin. "And Jack Chance can kiss my ass."

3

"YOU'RE GETTING MARRIED already?" At mid-morning Jack had walked into the large ranch kitchen in search of coffee, only to find Jack's stepmother, Sarah, and his brother Gabe knee-deep in wedding plans. Mary Lou Simms, the ranch cook, was in the thick of it, too, offering comments in between tending a huge pot of chili on the stove.

Gabe's truck hadn't been in the driveway earlier, but he was home now, looking scruffy and quite pleased with himself. Jack wasn't used to seeing his youngest brother unshaven, his dark blond hair sticking in twenty different directions. With luck Gabe was so besotted with his lady love that he'd forget to ask how Jack's evening had turned out.

"Morgan and I see no point in waiting." Gabe sat at the kitchen island drinking coffee with Sarah.

"And I'm glad for that." Sarah seemed giddy at the prospect. She'd always looked youthful, even though she'd let her hair go naturally white, but this morning she seemed almost girlish. "Your idea of having the ceremony on horseback means we don't have to decorate for the wedding, just for the reception."

"Horseback, huh?" Jack walked over to the hat rack in the corner of the kitchen.

"Morgan's game," Gabe said, "so I decided what the heck. Might as well take advantage of the famous Jackson Hole scenery."

"Now I can see the reason for rushing things." Jack hung his hat next to Gabe's. "An outdoor ceremony wouldn't work so well in the snow."

"Exactly," Sarah said. "Besides, it'll be a fun challenge to pull it together in...wow, less than two weeks."

"I'm glad you think so." Jack was happy that Gabe and Morgan were getting married. He was also pleased to see Sarah so excited about the wedding. But his own misery moved in like a dark cloud to cover any potential joy. He needed to snap out of this foul mood and get into the spirit of things.

Mary Lou left her chili to simmer, poured a mug of coffee and handed it to Jack. "I figure this is what you wandered in for."

"I did. Thanks." Maybe caffeine would help.

Mary Lou gestured with the carafe. "Gabe? Sarah?"

"Load me up." Gabe held out his mug. "Didn't get much sleep last night." He winked at Jack. "You don't look like you did, either."

"Not much." Actually, none.

"You boys." Mary Lou clucked in disapproval. "I

thought you'd both passed the stage of staying out 'til all hours. Sarah? Coffee?"

"Nothing for me, thanks. I'm wired as it is with all this good news." Her blue eyes shone as she flashed Jack a smile. "Did you see Josie last night?"

Jack glared at Gabe. Some people couldn't keep their traps shut.

Gabe shrugged. "She wanted the whole story. You know how moms are."

"Right." Jack really didn't know how moms were. Sometimes they were great, like his stepmother, Sarah, but other times they left. For years Sarah had asked Jack to call her Mom, but he liked calling her Sarah to distance her from the other mother he'd known, the one who'd deserted him.

"So *did* you see Josie?" Gabe asked.

Jack thought then how much alike Gabe and Sarah were—not only in looks, because they were both fair with blue eyes, but also in being such cheerful, curious people.

Sarah could keep a secret when she had to, though. Until a few weeks ago, she'd kept a whopper. Turned out Nick, Jonathan's middle son, wasn't hers. Instead he was the result of an affair that took place after Jonathan divorced Jack's mother and before he met Sarah.

But Nick had been raised at the ranch as Sarah's son, and finding out the truth of his birth had shattered his world. Thanks to his fiancée, Dominique, Nick was recovering from that emotional blow. The two of them were holding off on a wedding until Dominique transferred her photography business from Indiana to

Wyoming, but it looked as if two of the three Chance boys were settling down. As usual, Jack was the lone wolf, the son who didn't quite fit in.

"So? What's the deal with Josie?" Gabe was nothing if not persistent.

"I saw her for a little while," Jack said. "Her brother, Alex, is visiting." That was the God's truth, and it should stop their questions for a while.

"Tough luck," Gabe said with a twinkle in his eye.

"Whatever." He finished his coffee, set the mug in the sink, and reached for his hat. "I need to get back to work."

"There's one wedding detail to handle before you go," Gabe said.

"What's that?" Jack put on his hat in preparation for leaving as quickly as possible. Maybe he'd take a ride out to the north pasture and check the fence. Putting some distance between him and these wedding plans sounded good.

"I'd like it if you and Nick would share the job of best man. Would that work for you?"

"Sure. Be glad to." Sharing the job would be a relief. He wouldn't have to handle everything, and Nick was good at that sappy stuff.

"Excellent. Morgan's going to have two maids of honor, so it'll be balanced."

Jack nodded, not really listening. "Great. Well, if that's all, then—"

"You'll probably want a heads-up on who the maids of honor will be." Gabe had a gleam in his eye.

Jack hoped to hell Gabe wasn't hoping to promote

a romance between him and one of Morgan's sisters. There might be several to choose from, because Morgan had come from a family of seven kids.

He turned to make his getaway. "You can fill me in on the particulars later."

"I just thought you'd want to know that Morgan's asking Josie."

Jack froze. His brain froze, too. But when it thawed a couple of seconds later, horror poured out in torrents. No. He couldn't be in a wedding with Josie. That was completely unacceptable.

Doing his best to cover his reaction, he turned back to Gabe. "I'm surprised."

"You look more than surprised." Gabe's mouth twitched as if he dearly wanted to laugh. "You look like someone whacked you upside the head with a two-by-four."

"Why Josie? I thought Morgan had a passel of sisters and brothers."

"She does, but her sister Tyler's the only one she wants in the wedding party. Morgan and Josie have hit it off. I'm guessing Morgan's over there right now asking her. I figured you'd want to know, in case you're talking to Josie at some point."

Jack would rather not admit that he didn't expect to talk with Josie…ever. Gabe must assume they were back on speaking terms and Josie's brother had been the only obstacle to a happy reunion. This wasn't going to work, but he didn't know how to say that without revealing all his personal business in front of Sarah and Mary Lou.

Then he had a brilliant idea. "I thought you wanted to have this wedding on horseback."

"We do. Morgan's excited about it and it should make the planning a lot easier."

"Then Morgan might want to pick a different maid of honor. Josie doesn't ride."

Gabe's eyebrows lifted. "Are you sure?"

"Absolutely. She's never been on a horse in her life. We talked about me teaching her, but we never got around to it." Because they were so busy getting busy.

Sarah waved a hand. "Then that's the solution. She won't have to be an accomplished horsewoman for this, so you have plenty of time to teach her the basics before the wedding."

Dear God, he'd only made things worse. "I can't."

Sarah's gaze sharpened. "Of course you can."

Panic made him sound desperate. "No, really, Sarah. I have enough to do managing things around here, and now there's the best man stuff to think about. Riding lessons are out of the question."

Sarah and Gabe exchanged a glance. Jack knew that glance. He'd given himself away by protesting too loudly about the riding lessons.

"I'm sure we can work out a time," Sarah said. "After all, this is important."

Jack saw no way around it. He'd have to come clean. "The thing is, Josie won't want to take riding lessons from me."

Gabe's eyes narrowed. "Why not?"

"Last night I mistook her brother for a new boyfriend and I...sort of...attacked him."

Gabe and Sarah gasped and Mary Lou dropped a spoon on the stove with a loud clatter. All three of them stared at him as if he'd grown horns and a tail.

"He's not hurt or anything. As Gabe knows, I'd had a…a couple of drinks, so my aim was off."

Gabe's muffled snort meant he was trying hard not to laugh.

Sarah, however, looked scandalized. "You *assaulted* Josie's brother? I can't believe you did that."

"I can't, either," Mary Lou said. "That's not like you, Jack."

"It was a mistake."

Gabe's eyes were watering from his efforts to hold back his laughter. "No kidding." He cleared his throat. "This does put a different spin on things."

Jack sighed. "If Morgan has her heart set on Josie, then I'm sure the two of us can muddle through the wedding, but somebody else will have to teach her how to ride. Maybe one of the hands could do it."

"Maybe." Lips twitching, Gabe continued to assess him. "But are you sure you could handle that?"

"What do you mean? Of course I could. That's what I'm saying, isn't it? Get somebody else."

"Yeah, but last night you thought you had a rival and decided to take him down." Gabe looked as if he might be ready to burst out laughing. "I'd hate for you to go after one of our cowhands."

"Oh, for crying out loud! Just because I screwed up one time, that doesn't mean—"

"That you still consider Josie your woman? I think it

does." Gabe looked over at Sarah and Mary Lou. "What do you two think?"

"I think you need to make amends to Josie," Sarah said. "And you should do that before the wedding, so we don't have any unpleasantness spoiling Gabe and Morgan's big day. Teaching her to ride would be the perfect opportunity."

Mary Lou nodded. "Good idea."

"She won't go for it." Jack felt the trap closing around him. He'd known he would pay for last night's debacle, but he'd never dreamed it would be like this.

"She will if you present it the right way," Sarah said. "Tell her as one adult to another that the two of you need to iron out your differences in private so that you don't accidentally ruin Gabe and Morgan's wedding."

"You want *me* to approach her about this?" Jack couldn't even contemplate it.

Sarah continued her devastatingly logical argument. "If you can't do that, how do you expect to be able to make it through the wedding festivities? It's not just the ceremony, you know. We'll need a rehearsal the Friday afternoon before the wedding, and there will be a dinner on Friday night."

"She's right about this, bro." Gabe's voice held only a trace of pity. "You and Josie have to work through whatever's bothering you before the wedding."

Jack gave it one last shot. "I promise you that nothing will happen. You have my word on it."

"I'm sure Josie would promise, too," Gabe said, "but when it comes to tension between a man and a woman, all bets are off. I really want you there, and Morgan really wants Josie there. They've bonded."

"That seems kind of quick," Jack said.

"It makes sense. They're about the same age and they're both small business owners. And...they've each been involved with a Chance brother."

Jack made a dismissive noise low in his throat.

"I wondered if it would be a problem when Morgan suggested Josie," his brother said.

"Don't worry, Gabe." Sarah picked up her coffee mug. "Jack's going to take care of this when he teaches Josie to ride, aren't you, Jack?"

He couldn't see a way out of this corner they'd backed him into. "Yeah, I'll take care of it."

"Good." Sarah raised her mug in salute.

Jack thought she seemed way too happy about the riding lesson plan. But then, she hadn't disapproved of Josie the way his father had. In fact, Sarah had stood up for Josie a couple of times when his dad had made disparaging remarks.

"Oh, and thanks for telling me about her brother," Sarah added. "If he's staying awhile, we should invite him to the wedding."

"I'll find out his plans," Jack said. Oh, yes, he was going to pay for his moment of madness when he'd knocked on Josie's door and tried to deck her brother. He wondered how high the price would end up being. "In fact, I might as well drive into town now and get this program started."

"Might as well." Gabe sounded as cheerful as Sarah.

Strangely, Jack was feeling a little lighter, too. "See you all later." He touched the brim of his hat as he glanced at Sarah and Mary Lou.

"Bye, Jack!" Mary Lou beamed at him.

"And thanks," Sarah added.

"No problem." It would be, but he'd handle it with as much grace as possible. Maybe it wouldn't be so bad. He left the kitchen knowing full well that Gabe, Sarah and Mary Lou would discuss his situation with Josie the minute he was out of earshot.

As he walked down the hallway and into the living room with its beamed ceilings, gigantic rock fireplace and buckets of family memories, he thought about the irony of the situation. Sarah was forcing him to interact with Josie. When Jonathan was alive, he'd actively tried to discourage the relationship.

To be fair, his dad hadn't disliked Josie so much as he'd disliked the man Jack became after he'd started seeing her. Until then, Jack had been up with the sun every morning, helping his father and acting like a true rancher's son.

But Josie had changed all that. Jack had fallen into the habit of helping her close the bar and then spending the night with her. As a bar owner, Josie's hours were the opposite of a rancher's. She stayed up late and slept in. When Jack started keeping her schedule, Jonathan had let his displeasure be known.

Not about to be ordered around, Jack had continued his new routine. He'd argued with his father about it many times. Jonathan's insistence on getting the filly that fateful morning had been less about fetching the horse than about proving who was in charge. Jack hadn't wanted his dad to win, but the cost of that battle of wills had been too high.

Jack refused to get into a similar battle with Sarah. He'd do what she wanted, and if he could present the situation well enough to Josie, she would agree, too. As he left the ranch house and climbed into his truck, he realized Sarah had done him a favor. His pride wouldn't have allowed him to contact Josie, but this lesson scheme gave him an excuse. And despite his misgivings, he was glad for it.

4

JOSIE BARELY HAD TIME to wrap her head around Morgan's request that she be a maid of honor before she had to be downstairs taking a delivery of beer. Good thing her cook, Andy, was there to double-check everything, because Josie was having trouble concentrating.

All she could think about was this wedding coming up in less than two weeks, a wedding that would involve Jack. And horses. Morgan had promised her that the riding would be no big deal. Josie could go to any of a number of stables in the area and get some basic instruction.

The horseback riding didn't worry Josie all that much. She'd learned to ski as an adult, so she could learn to ride. In fact, a ski vacation had been her introduction to Jackson Hole.

She'd come back several times before realizing that if she truly intended to buy a bar, she wanted it to be in this area. And that decision had led to her meeting Jack Chance.

As the beer truck pulled away, she glanced at her watch. The bar opened for lunch at eleven-thirty, which gave her fifteen minutes to get her act together. At least someone else would be behind the bar. Josie turned the operation over to Tracy Gibbons on weekdays and she occupied herself with the computer in the office.

She had bills to pay and books to reconcile, but she wondered how much she'd accomplish when all she could think about was the darned wedding...and Jack. She would have loved to talk this over with Alex, but he'd left early in the morning to hike in the Tetons.

On second thought, she should decide how she planned to handle this turn of events before telling Alex. He might want to confront Jack, after all, now that his sister would be required to be in Jack's company for the better part of a weekend. Josie didn't want Alex and Jack to square off again. Once was enough.

So Alex would have to cool it, and somehow Josie would manage to get through the wedding without letting Jack know he'd ripped open the wound she'd been trying so desperately to heal. With a sigh of resignation, she walked through the back door of the bar into her tiny office and turned on the computer.

The scent of onions simmering in olive oil told her Andy had started cooking the lunch entrées. Usually by now she was hungry, but not today. Her tummy twisted in knots at the thought of eating. She'd have to get over her nerves in the next ten days, though, or she wouldn't be much good to Morgan as a maid of honor. The bride was the only one allowed to be nervous.

As she waited for the computer to load its various

programs, a gut-wrenchingly familiar knock sounded at the back door. She and Jack had devised a code so she'd know in advance it was him—three soft raps and two harder ones.

Ten months ago that rap would have been a signal to fling open the back door of the office and pull him in for a scorching kiss. Sometimes they'd gone beyond a mere kiss. On at least three occasions she'd locked both doors—the one to the outside and the one leading into the bar—and they'd had sex in her office.

This morning the door to the bar stood open and she could hear Andy banging around in the kitchen. Tracy would arrive any minute, along with any customers who liked to get an early start on their lunch or a midday beer.

She could imagine why Jack was here. Undoubtedly it had something to do with the wedding. And so it started, their required interaction. Taking a deep breath, she left her chair and opened the back door.

Ten months rolled away as her gaze swept over the cowboy standing there. His black hat shaded his eyes, making their dark depths look sexy and mysterious. His hat was slightly dusty. So was the rest of him, including a blue plaid western shirt, faded jeans and well-worn boots.

Jack hadn't spruced up for the occasion. He'd come straight from whatever work he'd been involved in this morning. The combined scent of leather and sweat had become an aphrodisiac to her during the months they were together, and it had lost none of its punch. Damn it all, she still wanted him with a ferocity that left her shaking.

But wanting him wasn't the only issue. Being alone with him filled her with nostalgia for the days when Jack had been her entire world. She'd been giddy with happiness, floating through her daily routine in anticipation of spending her nights with Jack. She had to believe that he'd enjoyed their time together just as much, because he'd used every possible excuse to be with her.

She took a long, restorative breath. "Is this about the wedding?" There, that sounded sufficiently curt and businesslike.

"Yes." His dark gaze flicked over her in much the same way she'd surveyed him.

She wished now that she'd taken more time with her hair, her clothes, her makeup. She'd thrown on an old pair of jeans, her most comfortable boots and a T-shirt that said—unfortunately—Save A horse; Ride A cowboy.

"I remember that shirt," Jack said.

She remembered doing exactly what the shirt recommended. But she wouldn't be repeating that with Jack, no matter how much she might want to.

They needed to stay on track here. "You wanted to talk to me about something concerning the wedding?"

"Uh, yeah. Right. We…that is…listen, can I come in and discuss it?"

"Sure." She stepped back to allow him to enter. She might as well test herself and see if she could handle being behind closed doors with him. It wasn't as if they'd be *really* alone, anyway. Andy was nearby and Tracy would be here any time now.

All that rationalization disappeared the minute she closed the door and turned to face him. Every kiss, every touch, every minute of lovemaking came back to her. If she'd hoped the attraction was manageable, she'd been dead wrong. She ached for what used to be.

Maybe if she took refuge behind her desk, that would help. She retreated to her own chair and motioned to an armless wooden one on the opposite side of the desk. She used it when interviewing employees. "Have a seat."

Typical Jack, he spun the chair around and straddled it, leaning his forearms on the back. He would have to sit like that. Dear God, why did his jeans have to fit so lovingly over his package?

He nudged his hat back with his thumb and gazed at her. "Looks like we'll have to deal with each other during the festivities."

"Guess so." His voice stroked her nerve endings. She picked up a pen and started clicking the mechanism before realizing how idiotic that looked. She threw it down. "I'm sure we can do that."

"I'm sure we can, too, but Gabe knew I went to your place last night, and I ended up having to tell him and Sarah what happened with your brother."

"Oh." Josie would have loved a video of that scene.

"So they're convinced that you and I are a potential powder keg that could blow in the middle of the celebration." Jack tapped his thumb idly against the back of the chair.

She knew how talented he was with that thumb. Yes, they might be a powder keg, but she feared the explosion would have to do with lust, not anger. Just sitting in this small office with Jack, her breathing had changed and her panties were damp. "They don't give us much credit for self-control, do they?"

"They might have if I hadn't thrown a punch at your brother. But after hearing about that, they've made a request, and I think we should honor it."

"I promised Morgan I'd be in the wedding, Jack. I can't go back on that promise."

"Nobody's asking you to. But Gabe and Sarah want some proof that we can get along like two civilized adults. So they figured if I was the one to teach you how to ride, then we'd work through our differences and be okay for the wedding."

"Are you insane? I don't want you to teach me how to ride. That's a disaster in the making." She'd never in a million years be able to keep her hands off him if they embarked on a project like that.

"No, it won't be a disaster. We'll make it work, and by the time the wedding rolls around, we won't be as likely to get teed off at each other."

He was a hottie, but he was an irritating hottie. "What's all this *we* stuff? I didn't throw a punch. Why don't you just say that they're worried about *you* and stop implying that it's my problem, too?"

He sighed. "All right. They're worried about me, but in order not to be worried, they've asked me to give you riding lessons."

"I've heard that cold showers can lower your testosterone level."

"Don't be a smart-ass. This is serious."

"No, it's not. It's silly. I'll behave myself during the wedding, and if you can't, then pop a Valium."

His gaze grew hot. "Look, I told them I'd do this, damn it. Just go along with it, okay?"

"Why should I?"

"You need to learn how to ride, for one thing."

"I'll do what Morgan suggested and use one of the stables. I don't want you teaching me to ride, Jack, and that's final." She could imagine it now. Him demonstrating a proper seat, her fixated on his buns, him astride the saddle, her wanting him astride her body.

"Why not?"

She'd take splinters under her fingernails before she'd tell him that. "Because you're bossy."

He nodded. "Fair enough. How about this? You'll be free to tell me to go to hell whenever I get too bossy."

"I've always felt free to tell you to go to hell."

A ghost of a smile flickered. "True."

That smile tugged at her heart. He used to smile all the time. They used to laugh and joke, even in bed.

Jack cleared his throat. "Tell you what. How about we try it for one lesson? If you really hate it, then we'll quit."

She could see he wanted her to agree, but she wasn't sure exactly why. Apparently he'd told Gabe and Sarah that he'd do this, so it might be a matter of pride, but she sensed something else, an eagerness that had nothing to do with his family's request.

"Why is this so important to you?"

"Well, I said I would, for one thing. But…" He paused and glanced down at his hands. "I've given you the impression I'm only interested in sex."

"It's more than an impression. You flat out said so in October."

He raised his head and gave her a soul-melting gaze. "I'd like a chance to correct that."

Oh, God. It was the one thing he could say that would make a difference. And when he looked at her like that, she couldn't refuse him anything. He probably knew it, probably had used his powerful charisma on purpose to get what he wanted.

Her pulse raced, but she did her best to appear bored with the subject. "All right, Jack."

Did he really intend to prove that he could be with her and not act on the sexual tension that had always existed between them, that existed even now, in this very room? And if he could be strong enough to resist temptation, could she?

Dismounting smoothly from the chair, he stood. "We should start with just an hour lesson."

She stood, too, but she didn't move from behind the desk. Too dangerous. "Just remember, it could be over in five minutes."

"It won't be."

She'd always found his confidence sexy and now was no exception. "If you say so."

"It'll be fine. Can you be out at the ranch at nine in the morning? I know that's early for you, but—"

"I'll be there. We might as well find out right away if this is a good idea or a colossal mistake."

He smiled, a full-out, genuine smile this time. "Thanks, Josie. I owe you one."

"You owe me several, cowboy."

"Understood." He pulled his hat forward and touched two fingers to the brim. "See you in the morning."

After he was gone, she sank back onto her chair with a groan, her whole body shaking. Heaven help her, she was going to spend an hour with Jack in the morning. And she could hardly wait.

JACK DROVE BACK to the ranch in a hell of a good mood. He couldn't remember the last time he'd felt this happy. Then again, maybe he could. Ten months ago he and Josie had rolled around in her bed until the wee hours, making love, having pillow fights, eating chips and salsa naked, and making love again.

They'd had fun other nights, too, but he particularly remembered that one. Or maybe it was so clear because of the horror of the next day. Memories of Josie were still tied up with his dad's death and he wondered if that would ever change.

Remorse continued to stab him whenever he thought about blowing off his dad's request in order to stay in bed with her. That angry phone conversation had been the last time he'd spoken with his father. When Jonathan died, he was bitterly disappointed in his oldest son. Jack expected to live with that guilt for a long, long time.

He also needed to do something about that filly. She hadn't been ridden since the accident. Although she'd escaped with only a few scratches, nobody had been able to bring themselves to ride her. Consequently she'd spent the past ten months either in her stall or out in the pasture.

That was a shame. She was a pretty brown and white Paint with good confirmation and the unfortunate name of Bertha Mae. It couldn't be shortened to initials, either. He thought of how something like that would make Josie laugh and smiled to himself.

He used to like making her laugh, because she put her whole body into it. He'd especially loved the sensation of Josie laughing when his cock was buried deep inside her.

As he considered the likelihood of having that experience again, his smile faded. No matter how desperately he still wanted Josie, he absolutely was not going to use these riding lessons as a way to get back in her bed. He was responsible for her thinking all he cared about was sex, but it bothered him. A lot.

They'd enjoyed sex, but it hadn't been the sole reason for getting together, despite what he'd told her. Josie meant more to him than that, and somehow he thought she should know.

Arrogant though it might seem, he'd unconsciously figured on hooking up with Josie again someday, when he was ready. And he'd thought she would take him back if he apologized for his behavior. Yeah, that was extremely arrogant. Knowing that she might never take him back had brought him down a considerable number of pegs.

Jack pulled into the outbuilding designated as the

truck barn. The morning was pretty well shot, giving him a scant thirty minutes or so to work. Lunch was a big deal at the Last Chance, and Jack generally tried to be there.

Fifty years ago, his grandpa Archie had established a tradition that the hands ate lunch with the family. The other two meals were served to them in the bunkhouse, but everybody came up to the main house for lunch. Eventually the family dining room had become pretty crowded, so when Jonathan added the left wing to the house, Sarah had insisted on a space specifically for big gatherings.

With four round tables that sat eight, the room accommodated all the hands, and was also useful whenever potential buyers came to look over the ranch's registered Paints. Lunch had always been a high point of Jack's day until he'd started dating Josie. Then it had become an opportunity for his dad to comment on his neglected duties.

But today Jack looked forward to the meal, both for the chili Mary Lou had made this morning, and the success he'd be able to report to Gabe and Sarah. First, though, he would pay Bertha Mae a visit. Maybe this afternoon he'd carve out time to work with her.

Pocketing his truck keys, he walked down to the barn. Nick's dogs, Butch and Sundance, were sprawled on each side of the barn door, so Nick must be inside doing his veterinarian thing. His brother had found the dogs wandering along the road a couple of years ago, both looking scraggly. Now Butch's tan and white coat shone and Sundance's long black hair was free of burrs.

Jack gave each dog a scratch behind the ears before walking into the cool interior of the barn. "Nick, you in here?"

Nick's voice came from a nearby stall. "Yeah. Doing a routine checkup on Calamity Sam."

Postponing his visit to Bertha Mae, Jack made a side trip to the stall Calamity Sam shared with his mother, Calamity Jane. Both mother and two-month-old foal were gray and white Paints. "How's he doing?"

"Great." Nick glanced up as Jack leaned his forearms on the stall door. "Healthy as a—"

Jack groaned, drowning out the rest of the tired cliché that had become a permanent family joke. Horses were a lot more delicate than they looked, and the smallest little thing, such as a bad batch of grain, could kill them in no time. Raising horses was much more of a challenge than running cattle, which might be one of the reasons his dad had gradually phased out the cattle to specialize in Paints, and then decided to train them as cutting horses. Jonathan Chance had relished a challenge.

Nick ran a practiced hand over Calamity Sam's neck and gave the foal a pat before closing up his vet bag. "This is going to be a money horse."

"I hope so." Jack moved away from the stall door so Nick could come out.

"Count on it." Nick grabbed his hat from a hook and glanced at Jack as he put it on. "How'd it go with Josie this morning?"

Irritation pricked his good mood as he pictured Gabe spreading the word. Jack hated having his private business made public. "Does every blessed soul on the ranch know about it?"

"Pretty much everybody." Something about Nick's green eyes had always made him look as if he'd been up to no good, but they were especially full of the devil now. "Come on, Jack. You've been riding us hard for months. Don't blame the guys for enjoying this."

"What do you mean by *enjoying?*"

"There's a pool going as to whether Josie will agree to take those riding lessons from you."

Jack blew out a breath. "And I suppose you're in it."

"Hell, yes, I'm in it. I put in a long-distance call to Dominique so she could be, too. We both bet against you convincing Josie to do it."

"Nice. Thanks for the vote of confidence, Nick."

"Once you factor in the incident where you tried to deck her brother, it's the reasonable bet to make."

"Everybody knows about that?" Jack's eyes narrowed. "I'm gonna kill Gabe."

"Then you might as well go after Mary Lou and Mom, because they did their share of getting the word out. So, did she shoot you down? I have a twenty riding on this, bro."

"No, she did not shoot me down." At least Jack had the satisfaction of proving the naysayers wrong. But suddenly lunch didn't sound like such a good idea. On the other hand, if he didn't show up, no telling what rumors would be circulated about him.

"She went for it? I guess you haven't lost your touch, after all." Nick punched him lightly on the shoulder.

"Way to go, big brother. It's good to see you back in the game."

"I'm not *back in the game,* as you put it. I'm giving her riding lessons, period. Nothing more than that."

Nick smiled. "Yeah, sure. Strictly platonic."

"That's right."

"Keep telling yourself that, buddy. Keep telling yourself that."

Jack vowed that he would. He would show Josie— hell, he would show *everybody*—that Jack Chance could spend time with a woman and not have it be all about sex.

5

THE NEXT MORNING, Josie drove down the rutted dirt road leading to the ranch with her stomach in knots and Alex's warnings ringing in her ears. Her brother had not been happy that she'd agreed to take even one riding lesson from Jack.

Alex had volunteered to come along with her, but she'd convinced him not to. Before he'd left for another day of hiking, he'd cautioned her to be careful because this lesson was probably Jack's evil plan to lure her back into bed.

She couldn't admit to Alex, and could barely admit to herself, that she almost hoped it was. She'd missed Jack, both in bed and out of it. He probably wasn't good for her, but being celibate for months couldn't be good for her, either.

When she'd had virtually no contact for ten months, she'd been able to convince herself that she was better off without him. His stunt two nights ago had been ludicrous, and she'd done her best to put another black mark beside his name because of it. But then he'd come into her office yesterday bringing with him all that sex appeal and contrition. She'd fought the good fight, tried to be snarky, clever and dismissive, but in the end she'd caved.

She'd been fascinated to hear him claim that sex wouldn't be part of this arrangement, as if he had something to prove to her. Josie hadn't told Alex that. He might have insisted it was a ploy to throw her off her guard.

But none of that mattered now, because she'd arrived at the ranch. Her pulse rate jumped when she spotted Jack down by the barn standing beside two saddled horses tied to a hitching post.

A few other cowboys were in the area, but Josie couldn't seem to focus on anybody besides Jack. He'd worn her favorite black shirt—she'd told him it made him look like a gunslinger, especially paired with the black hat he loved. As always, his lean hips were tucked into a worn pair of jeans that she knew from experience would be soft as a baby's blanket from being washed so often.

Jack made quite the picture standing beside his large black and white Paint, but she needed to stop ogling him and get this show on the road. A couple of pickups were parked beside the barn, so she drove her Bronco down there and pulled in next to them.

She'd dressed with care for this riding lesson. Fortunately she had all the right clothes. Despite knowing nothing about riding, she'd wanted to fit in with the cowboy culture and had bought boots, jeans, western shirts and even a hat that lay brim-side up on the seat beside her.

Early on she'd learned that cowboys—and cowgirls— cherished their hats and were particular about how they were treated. No self-respecting cowboy would leave his hat for long brim-side down. A good hat belonged on a rack or brim-side up, to protect the shape the owner had given it.

Picking up her gray Stetson, she left her keys in the ignition and climbed out of the Bronco. She settled her hat on her head as she walked over toward Jack. Jack the horseman. Amazing though it seemed now, she'd never seen him ride.

Picturing him mounted on that black and white Paint, his snug jeans defining all his attributes as his thighs gripped the saddle, Josie grew faint with desire. At that moment, she realized that Jack would have to be the gatekeeper when it came to forgoing sex. Faced with his manly self in full cowboy mode, she simply wouldn't have the willpower.

His dark gaze gave nothing away as he glanced at her. "You're right on time." He gave no indication that he'd noticed she had on her sexiest jeans and a fitted shirt.

She'd chosen the outfit carefully, because whether he made a move or not, she hoped he'd want to. If he wanted to and exercised great restraint, that was kind of an exciting prospect. She liked being forbidden fruit.

"I told you I'd be here." She sounded crustier than she felt. Inside she was one gooey marshmallow of unsatisfied need.

"Okay, then." He pulled the brim of his black hat down over his eyes. "We can start in the corral if you want, but Destiny's a very calm gelding, so I think you'll be fine if we go out on the trail."

She managed to tear her gaze away from Jack long enough to look at the horse he'd chosen for her—a tall brown and white Paint with a white blaze down his nose. "So his name's Destiny?"

"I chose him for his disposition, not his name. He's twenty-two, and both Gabe and Nick learned to ride on him. He's as close to a pet as any horse on the ranch."

"Who named him Destiny?"

"I did, but don't hold that against me. I was ten and into dramatic names."

"Okay." She should know better than to assign sentimental motives to a guy like Jack. "What's your horse's name?" She couldn't believe she didn't know after all the time she'd spent with him.

"Bandit."

At the sound of his name, the horse turned his head and displayed the reason for it. The pattern of black and white on his face made him look as if he wore a mask.

"I see," Josie said. "What a perfect horse for a gunslinger. Thanks for wearing my favorite black shirt, by the way."

"It happened to be clean."

She didn't believe that for a minute. "I'm sure that's true, Jack. Heaven forbid you'd wear a certain shirt because you know I like it."

"Wouldn't dream of it." But there was a definite smile

in his voice. "Okay, what do you say we get this party started?"

"Fine with me." She looked up at the saddle, which seemed fairly high above the ground. "How do I get on?"

"From the left. Put your left foot in the stirrup, grab the saddle horn, and swing your right leg over."

Josie did as she was told and found herself astride a horse for the first time in her life. She was reminded of her first time on a chair lift at a ski resort—beginning something new was both scary and exhilarating.

"Take your feet out of the stirrups for a minute. They're a couple of inches too long."

Holding tight to the leather saddle horn, she glanced down at Jack as she slipped her feet out of the stirrups. He messed with the buckle on the left stirrup and kept brushing her leg in the process. She could have moved it out of the way, but she chose not to. His touch gave her the kind of shivers she hadn't felt in ten months.

He finished with the left stirrup and walked around the back of the horse to repeat the same procedure on the right one. Josie could swear his breathing had changed.

"Try that." His voice was as calm as ever, but he didn't look at her.

"How's it supposed to feel?"

He glanced up at her then, and his gaze was a lot more intense than it had been earlier. "It should feel…" His voice grew husky. "It should feel good."

Her breath caught. "I don't know what good feels like."

Groaning softly, he squeezed his eyes shut. "Damn, Josie."

"I'm talking about the saddle."

He opened his eyes and looked into hers. "No, you're not, and neither am I."

Heat sluiced through her.

"Maybe we should stay in the corral," he said.

"Sounds boring."

"Sounds safe. You've never ridden before, so walking around the corral is probably the best—"

"I'd rather ride on the trail."

He gave her a long look. "All right. Then let's check your stirrups so we can get going. Stand up. There should be daylight between the saddle and your...and you." He swore softly again and looked away. "You know what I mean."

"Yes." She pressed the balls of her feet into the stirrups and rose up. "How's that?"

"Fine."

"You didn't look."

"Yeah, I did. You just didn't see me." He untied the reins from the hitching post, knotted them together, and lifted them over Destiny's head. "Hold these in your left hand."

She took them from him and their hands brushed. Once again her nerve endings played "The Hallelujah Chorus."

As if he needed some distance, Jack stepped back to deliver further instructions. "This horse neck reins. That means you lay the reins on his left side and he'll veer right, and vice-versa."

"Got it. How do I make him stop?"

"Say whoa and pull back gently and evenly on the reins. It won't take much. He has a soft mouth." Then, as if he couldn't help himself, Jack looked up at Josie's mouth.

Acting without thinking, she ran her tongue over her suddenly dry lips. Jack kept staring at her mouth, and she found herself leaning forward.

No telling what might have happened next if a rugged-looking cowboy who appeared to be in his late fifties hadn't called out from the doorway of the barn. "Hey, Jack, I'm going to run into town and pick up a couple of new shovels."

Jack blinked and gave his head a little shake before turning. "That's fine, Emmett."

"Oh, and have a nice ride, Josie," Emmett said. "You'll like Destiny. He has an easy gait, like sitting on a rocking chair."

"Thanks, Emmett." Josie recognized him now. He was Emmett Sterling, the ranch foreman. Every once in a while he came into the Spirits and Spurs for a beer, but he usually kept to himself so Josie had never had a conversation with him.

"I doubt I'll be back in time for lunch," Emmett said. "Unless you have an objection, I'll stop by the Bunk and Grub on the way home and check out a drainage problem in Pam's vegetable garden."

Jack smiled. "No problem. Have fun."

"It's not like that, Jack. I'm just being neighborly, is all."

"I understand, Emmett. We surely don't want Pam thinking we're a bad neighbor. I'm glad you're on the job."

Emmett snorted and waved a dismissive hand before heading for one of the two trucks parked beside the barn.

As Jack untied Bandit, he lowered his voice so only Josie could hear. "He's sweet on Pam, but he won't admit it."

"Why not?" Josie was very fond of Pam, who owned a local B and B. "She's wonderful, and they're about the same age."

"She's also loaded, and Emmett has some very old-fashioned ideas about money."

"That's too bad."

"They might work it out yet." Gathering the reins in one hand, he swung effortlessly up on his horse. "Ready?"

Oh, yeah. It wasn't the prospect of a horseback ride that had her quivering like a bowlful of jelly. When she looked at Jack sitting astride that magnificent black and white Paint like some dark warrior of old, she was ready for whatever he had in mind. She sat staring at him in total awe.

Jack's horse danced around and tossed his white mane while Destiny simply stood as if planted in the dirt. Josie didn't care a bit. She was content to watch Jack's thigh muscles contract under the soft denim of his jeans. She could focus on that all day long.

"You have to nudge him with your heels to make him go," Jack said gently.

"Oh." Josie gave Destiny a little prod. The horse headed in the direction he was pointed, toward the open barn door.

"Rein him to the right!" Jack called out.

Josie tried to remember how to do that, but for some reason Destiny just kept walking toward the barn.

"Here." Jack trotted over and took hold of the horse's bridle on the right side. "This way, son." He steered Destiny around and kept a grip on his bridle until they were past the barn and moving across a meadow filled with wildflowers. Ahead loomed a dirt trail that led into the trees. The trail was only wide enough for one horse at a time.

Josie had no chance to admire the wildflowers. She gripped the saddle horn with both hands. She'd looped the reins around one wrist, but no one would accuse her of directing this horse in any fashion. Her foot slipped out of the right stirrup and she used the toe of her boot to try and get it back.

"Let me." He stopped both horses, then leaned down and held Josie's stirrup until she had her foot back in it.

"I feel like a total klutz."

"It's your first time." He grinned at her. "Go easy on yourself. After all, you're a horseback-riding virgin."

She rolled her eyes. "And here I thought my virginal days were behind me."

"Don't worry. I'll be gentle."

It was the sort of banter they'd specialized in when they'd been a couple, and they slipped into it naturally, maybe too naturally. Their ease with each other had been one of the most seductive parts of the relationship. Josie could be herself with Jack. She could let down her hair, both literally and figuratively.

But then he'd blindsided her by leaving abruptly last fall. She'd do well to remember that.

"Nudge him with your heels again," Jack said. "I want you to ride down the trail ahead of me so I can observe your technique."

Josie did as she was told and Destiny moved ahead of Jack and Bandit. "You want to observe my ass, is what you mean," she said over her shoulder. She probably shouldn't have made that remark, but old habits died hard.

"Cut it out, Josie. I'm trying very hard to behave myself."

She let go of the saddle horn with her right hand so she could get a better grip on the reins. "My brother thinks you set up this ride to seduce me."

"Your brother would nail my hide to the side of the barn if he could."

"I think so, yes."

"I don't blame him."

A thrill shot through her. "Are you admitting you set this up to seduce me, after all?"

"No, just the opposite. You're totally safe with me."
Damn.

"And for the record, I didn't set this up," he continued. "I'm doing it because Gabe and Sarah asked me. But now that I'm into it, I promise you there's no seduction plan."

Double damn. She believed him, though. Jack might have acted like a heel by breaking up with her on the phone ten months ago, but he wasn't a liar.

"Then I guess you'd better give me some riding instruction, Jack."

"I was about to. Keep your heels down if you don't want to lose your stirrups again."

She angled her feet so her heels were lower than her toes. "Better?"

"Much better. How're you doing?"

"Okay." She found the rhythmic motion of the horse to be quite erotic, but she chose not to tell him. If he could keep secrets, so could she. If a girl concentrated on a certain cowboy riding a horse directly behind her, and angled her pelvis a little bit forward, she might be able to get just the right pressure to...mmm. Nice.

"You're leaning forward too much. Sit back in the saddle and grip with your legs."

Spoilsport. It occurred to Josie that she'd neglected her sex life since the day Jack had ended their relationship. She'd found it easier to close herself off and enter a mental nunnery.

But Jack was back, even if he swore they wouldn't be getting horizontal. His presence in her life had awakened her sleeping sexuality, and fantasies were swirling in her head. She wondered if he still kept a condom tucked in the back pocket of his jeans. During their time together he'd never left home without it.

From the meadow, the trail entered a stand of pine and aspen with a little oak mixed in. Josie wondered if Jack had planned this ride so that they'd be in a secluded area. The dappled sunlight and trill of birds would make a nice backdrop for two naked people pumping away on a blanket.

Wow, had she actually thought that? She needed to get off that train immediately. Much more of that kind of fantasy and she'd be suggesting the activity to Jack.

He'd made it clear he wouldn't try to seduce her, so for her to suggest getting naked would be wrong on so many levels. She'd come off as both needy and pathetic.

"You're looking comfy up there," Jack said. "I think you're ready for a trot."

"Isn't that the bouncy thing?"

"Not if you sit back nice and easy and move with the horse. Kick your heels into Destiny's flanks and he'll trot for you."

Reasoning that a new challenge would get her mind off sex, she dug her heels into the horse's ribs. The result was less than optimal. Instead of rolling along with Destiny's ambling walk, Josie was suddenly sitting on top of a jackhammer.

She grabbed the saddle horn as her teeth clicked together and her fanny slapped repeatedly against the smooth leather beneath her. Spanking fantasies weren't part of her repertoire, and she wasn't amused. "I don't like this, Jack!"

He sounded completely unmoved by her plight. "Sit back in the saddle and let yourself feel the rhythm of the horse."

She tried, but she still bounced all over creation. "This...rhythm...doesn't...work...for me."

"Then bypass the trot and go straight into a canter."

"How?"

"Kick him again."

"Is there…a gearshift…in his…ribs?"

Jack laughed, which she thought was extremely impolite, so she kicked Destiny with a little more force than she'd intended. She felt the great muscles gather beneath her, and then she was flying through the forest at a speed that turned the landscape into a glorious blur.

Although she lost her hat, she somehow kept her feet in the stirrups, and she pressed down on them. *Now* she could match her rhythm to the horse's plunging gait, and she leaned forward, clutching the saddle horn with both hands, too excited to be scared. So *this* was riding!

The wind buffeted her ears, making her deaf to all sounds but her own rapid breathing. In her peripheral vision she saw a flash of black and white through the trees, and then Jack was in front of her, blocking her way as he slowed his horse, which forced Destiny to slow.

Finally, Jack pulled his horse to a halt, vaulted off, and dropped the reins to the ground. Walking quickly back to Destiny, he hauled Josie from the saddle so abruptly that he knocked his hat to the ground. "Are you okay? God, Josie, I didn't mean for you to make him run! You must have been terrified!"

Laughing, she shook her head. "I loved it." Reaching up, she ran her fingers through his tousled hair. "You'd better pick up your hat. I know how you feel about that Stetson of yours."

"Forget the hat."

"Forget it? Are you crazy?"

"No doubt. Josie, forgive me."

"For that wild ride? It was fun!"

"Not for the wild ride. For this." And he kissed her.

6

TWENTY MINUTES into the riding lesson, and Jack had already broken his vow to keep his hands off Josie. But when Destiny ran off with her, he panicked, frantic at the thought that she could get hurt. But she hadn't been hurt, and he was so damned grateful that he just needed…her mouth…good Lord, her mouth… He feasted with the hunger of a man who'd denied himself far too long.

If she'd pulled back or resisted in any way, he might have found the strength to stop this nonsense. Instead she opened that glorious mouth of hers and cupped the back of his head in both hands to hold him fast.

Josie. So warm, so incredibly soft and yielding in his arms. He didn't deserve this melting acceptance, but he couldn't stop himself from taking it. They'd perfected this dance through hours of practice, and he slid back into the familiar wonder of kissing Josie as if he'd done it yesterday.

But he hadn't kissed her yesterday. For ten long, bleak months he'd been without this incredible experience.

During the time they'd been together he'd developed some self-control so that he could hold her and kiss her without needing to rip her clothes off immediately. In ten months of celibacy, that self-control had disappeared.

Instantly he was on fire, his heart pounding and his cock hard. He moaned and pulled her in tight, wanting her with a fierceness that threatened to overwhelm every decent intention he possessed.

Josie was no help at all. Molding herself so his straining erection fit into the vee of her thighs, she whimpered against his mouth. That familiar sound reminded him of all the special sounds she made when he drove her crazy. He wanted to hear her pant, and moan, and beg, and cry out his name when he gave her an orgasm, and yell when he gave her another, and…

Something, or someone, bumped him from behind. His first thought was that Josie's brother had arrived and was ready to beat the tar out of him. Reluctantly he ended the kiss and glanced over his shoulder.

Destiny nudged him again, harder this time.

Jack didn't know whether to laugh or swear.

"Jack?"

He gazed down into gray eyes that had gone all soft and dreamy. She would let him make love to her right now if he asked. After all those months together, he knew her moods. But he'd made a vow not to let sex be a part of this project.

"Destiny's a bit spoiled from his years of being around kids," he said. "He doesn't like to be ignored, so he's reminding me that he's here."

Josie searched Jack's expression a moment before

easing away from him. "Considering your plan of non-involvement, that's probably a good thing, huh?"

"Yeah." He blew out a breath and tried to get his bearings. All he really knew was that his arms felt very empty without her in them.

Well, served him right for screwing things up so quickly. "I'm not going to make excuses. I shouldn't have done that."

"And I shouldn't have let you." Mischief danced in her eyes. "Want to do it again?"

He groaned. "Don't tempt me."

"Hey, you started it." She shoved her hands in the back pockets of her jeans and stuck out her chest, which made her look adorably defiant and sexy as hell. "I was just out here taking a riding lesson when you decided to play tonsil hockey. Can I help it if you put ideas in my head?"

"You're right." Glancing around, he found his hat in the dirt, picked it up, and dusted it off. "It was completely my fault."

"Damn straight." Her tone softened. "I wonder if we're attempting the impossible, Jack. How are we supposed to act like casual friends after being lovers?"

"I don't know." Destiny bumped him again. He turned and swatted the horse on the nose with his hat. "Behave."

Destiny stretched out his neck and nuzzled Jack's hip pocket, obviously looking for a treat.

"Hey, stop!" Jack stepped aside and took the horse by the bridle. "No treats. You have some bad habits, son."

Josie smiled. "We're not so different from that horse, you know."

"What do you mean?"

"We have the bad habit of expecting sex when we're together."

"That's ridiculous." He tapped his hat against his thigh. "We're thinking human beings, not trained animals. We can exercise restraint."

"Oh, really?" Her eyebrows arched.

"Just because I kissed you doesn't mean I have to keep doing it."

"Then I guess you're stronger than I am, because now that you've kissed me, all I can think about is having sex with you."

Heat rolled through him in waves. "I wish you hadn't said that."

"You might as well know the truth. It's not like I'll be able to hide it from you. We understand each other too well." She pointed a finger at him. "And don't think I can't read you just as easily. Right this minute you're wishing you could back me up against the nearest flat surface and do me, but you're too stubborn to admit it."

He should get a medal for self-control, because the more she talked, the more he wanted exactly that. Good thing he no longer carried an emergency condom like he used to do when they were together. That helped. Still, he could imagine a few things they could do that wouldn't require a condom.

He clutched Destiny's bridle to keep from reaching for her. "Even if that's true, and I'm not saying it is, I said I wouldn't have sex with you, and I intend to keep my word."

Josie rolled her eyes. "Very noble of you. If that's how you feel, then let's forget the riding lessons, because I don't want to put myself through this."

"Through what?"

"Hello? Sexual frustration! I don't care to watch your sexy buns warming the seat of your saddle if the bakery is permanently closed, okay? Let's just give up on this whole program. We'll muddle through the wedding as best we can under the circumstances."

Giving up wasn't something Jack looked favorably on, and in this case, everybody and his brother—and *hers*—would know about it. "Giving up isn't an option."

"I'm sorry, but you don't have control over whether we give up. May I remind you that I do."

"But, Josie—"

"Don't *but, Josie* me! Maybe if you hadn't kissed me, I'd have an easier time of it, but the fact remains that you did kiss me, and now I'm primed and ready to rumba. However, if I stay away from you for the next week or so, I'll get over it."

If he lived to be a hundred and fifty, Jack would never understand women. He let go of Destiny's bridle and gestured with his hat. "Now let me get this straight. The other night, you thought I was some kind of horn dog to show up at your place on the spur of the moment. You made it clear you were finished with me and my sex-crazed behavior. Now you're perfectly willing to get horizontal. What's changed?"

She blew out a breath. "I've already told you, but apparently it didn't make an impression. You kissed me."

"And you can't just forget about that?"

"No, I can't." She folded her arms. "Can you?"

"I don't know, but I'm willing to try for the good of all concerned. We need to demonstrate we can get along, and the riding lessons are supposed to—"

"Have you considered that there's another option?"

"Like what?"

"First of all, we continue with the riding lessons and expand them to two hours. You can tell everyone I'm a slow learner." Her gray eyes sparkled.

He knew that look, and it usually meant he needed to be cautious. "You're not a slow learner. You have natural athletic ability, and it won't take much instruction for you to be a decent rider."

"Good to hear. Because, unbeknownst to everyone else, we'll be using all our spare time for sex."

IF ONLY SHE HAD a camera. His expression was absolutely priceless. Jack had always been proud of his ability to keep his reactions to himself, and consequently she liked making a game of trying to shock him into revealing his true feelings.

She'd succeeded this morning. His dark eyes widened in obvious disbelief, but that disbelief soon gave way to excitement. No doubt his quick mind was already imagining the possibilities.

Yet he hesitated. "That isn't the way everything was supposed to go." He sounded both hopeful and confused. "I promised you—hell, I promised *myself* that we wouldn't have sex."

There it was again, a hint of vulnerability, as if he cared what she'd think if he broke that promise. It touched her more than a little. Maybe these past ten months had worked some changes in him, after all.

"I know," she said softly. "I'm the one suggesting we change the plan, not you."

He looked down at the hat in his hand and brushed a leaf from the crown. Then he glanced up. "You're planning to keep this a secret from your brother?"

She didn't feel great about that, but telling Alex would only cause more problems. "I don't see any reason for him to know. I don't think anyone has to know, actually. That way we won't get any unsolicited advice on whether this is a wise move or not."

"It probably isn't." Yet he hung his hat on Destiny's saddle horn and moved toward her.

"Probably not." She held his gaze, knowing he intended to kiss her again and knowing that she needed that more than she needed air.

"So would you call this a stopgap measure?" He advanced another step.

"Exactly." Her heart beat faster the nearer he came. "It's a temporary fix to get us through the wedding, so we don't have a bunch of messy sexual tension going on. After that…" She wasn't sure what came after that.

"Maybe we shouldn't worry about what comes after that." He stood barely a foot away, his heat calling out to her. "Maybe we should take it one day at a time."

"Good idea." The intensity of his gaze made her

quiver. "Our goal…" She swallowed. "Our goal is to make it through the wedding. Then we'll see."

"And in the meantime we'll fit in as much sex as we can?"

"That was my thought."

Slowly and deliberately, he pulled her into his arms. "I like the way you think."

But when his mouth came down on hers, she wasn't thinking at all, just feeling. For six months, kissing Jack had been among her favorite activities, and she'd missed it terribly. She loved the way Jack kissed, loved being held in those strong arms, and especially loved the melting sensation as he drove her slowly insane.

When she kissed Jack, she forgot everything but this—the wanting and the promise of pleasure. Her body hummed with delight as he cupped her bottom and pulled her close. Mmm, yes. She wanted what was under that soft denim, and she wanted it now.

He lifted his lips a fraction from hers, and his warm breath carried the scent of the mint toothpaste he liked. "It can't be now."

She wiggled against him to demonstrate that they were both prepped for this encounter. "That's not what the rest of you says."

He nibbled at her mouth. "The rest of me has nothing to wear for the occasion."

She couldn't hold back a sigh of disappointment. "But I thought you always carried—"

"Not since we broke up."

"Now I feel special."

"You always have been, Josie."

Her heart squeezed. She'd needed to hear that.

He ran his tongue over her lower lip. "I could do something nice for you, though."

"Nuh-uh." She reached between them and caressed the length of him through his jeans. "I want the whole enchilada, so to speak."

He nuzzled behind her ear. "Then you'll have to wait."

She groaned. "Maybe…maybe you could unbutton my blouse."

"I could do that." With practiced ease he unfastened the snaps and slipped his hand inside to cup her lace-covered breast. He stroked her through the fabric. "Feels like the cream-colored one."

She arched into his palm as she reveled in having his hands on her again. "Wrong. You've never seen this one. It's pink."

"Then I have to look." Drawing back, he opened her shirt. "Very nice." He fingered the front clasp and looked into her eyes. "Still holding out for the whole enchilada?"

"Maybe you could undo my bra."

His mouth curved in a slow smile as he flipped the catch.

"Don't look so superior, Jack Chance, like you're all that and a bag of chips."

He shook his head as he moved the bra aside and lifted her breasts in both hands. "I'm not, but you are." He brushed his thumbs lazily over her nipples and watched them tighten. "I've missed touching you, Josie."

She closed her eyes as sensations shot from her nipples to her womb. "I haven't missed you at all."

"Liar."

"But as long as you're here, maybe you could…"

"I was hoping you'd ask." Leaning down, he circled her nipple with his tongue.

"That's very…pleasant."

He raised his head. "Pleasant's not good enough." Wrapping her in his strong arms, he lifted her up and took her nipple more firmly into his mouth.

How she loved those he-man tactics. Only a man with a physical job like his would have the strength to lift and hold her while he enjoyed the bounty of her breasts. After Jack, she was completely ruined for wimps. She wrapped her legs around his hips and abandoned herself to the joy of his mouth and tongue.

But gripping her legs tight around him made her aware of the hot ache in the part of her pressed up against his belt buckle. She'd wanted the whole enchilada, and that would have been wonderful if Jack still carried an emergency condom. But knowing he'd only done that when he was with her really did make her feel special. She couldn't fault him for not having one now. He'd meant well.

But the longer he played with her breasts, the more tension built inside her, causing her to want his attentions to be a little more specific. She might have to settle for less than she'd originally hoped for. "Jack…"

"Hmm?" He paused in the middle of his most excellent caress.

"Maybe…you could undo my belt and unzip my jeans."

His low, triumphant chuckle should have irritated her, but she was too far gone. As he eased her back onto her feet and unfastened her belt, she held on to his shoulders and whimpered. "Hurry."

"I will. Just don't go ahead without me."

She might, she realized. The moment he shoved his hand inside her panties, a spasm hit. "Oh, Jack."

"I've got you." With his other hand splayed against the small of her back, he pushed deep with two fingers and pressed his thumb against her clit.

A few quick strokes with those talented fingers and she came, crying out in relief and gratitude.

"Look at me, Josie." He rotated his thumb over her flash point.

She lifted her eyes to his as tension coiled inside her again.

"Once more." He began an easy rhythm, sliding his fingers back and forth, creating a sound both erotic and elemental. "It's been a long time."

"Yes." Her voice was breathy, her willpower entirely gone. No one had ever brought out this kind of abandon in her until Jack. He awakened something primitive in her psyche, and she surrendered to it once again, letting him stroke her body to readiness as his dark eyes made love to her soul.

She moaned as the moment drew closer.

"Good?"

"You know it is."

"Tomorrow, I want my mouth there."

The mere suggestion catapulted her into another climax. She arched her back and gasped his name. He held her steady as the tremors rolled through her.

"That's it," he murmured. "Let go. Let go."

And she did. She let go of her anger, her fears and her inhibitions. Jack had that effect on her. Tomorrow she might decide indulging her craving for him was a really stupid idea. But for today, she felt sensuous, fulfilled and gloriously free.

That couldn't be all bad.

7

JACK WAS EXTREMELY GRATEFUL that no one happened to be around the barn area when he and Josie rode in. He wasn't sure how someone else might interpret Josie's pink cheeks, unruly hair and wrinkled clothes, but he'd rather not find out. Josie was safely in her Bronco and headed back toward town when Gabe rode up on Finicky, a chocolate and white Paint he used for cutting horse competitions.

"How'd it go?" Gabe dismounted and wrapped Finicky's reins around the hitching post.

"Fine." As Jack pulled off Destiny's saddle and saddle blanket, he thought about Josie climbing back on Destiny after she'd done up her clothes.

She'd wiggled in the saddle and smiled down at him. "I'd rather ride you," she'd said with a wink. "So don't forget the condoms, cowboy."

As if he would. All his noble intentions had been swept away by the prospect of having sex with Josie every morning for a week. He'd already thought of all the secluded places within a half hour's ride. A couple of spots were only about fifteen minutes from the barn, which would give them bonus time.

"Hey, Jack."

"What?" He glanced up to find Gabe staring at him.

"I don't mean to tell you your business, but you just took the saddle off that horse. I'm a little confused as to why you turned around and put it back on. Destiny looks a little confused, too."

Heat climbed up from Jack's shirt collar. Sure enough, he'd re-saddled Destiny and was busily tightening the cinch. The horse regarded him with curiosity.

Jack reached for an explanation—any explanation. "I remembered as I took this saddle off that the cinch wasn't quite right, like something was ripping loose. I wanted to check it out."

"That's usually best done in the tack room."

"I like doing it on the horse." He made a great show of crouching down and examining the cinch and buckle from all sides. "Looks okay, after all." He gave Destiny a pat. "Thanks, son."

Gabe's snort of laughter told Jack he hadn't fooled his brother.

"A little distracted, are we, Jack?" Gabe unsaddled Finicky.

"It's possible." Jack did his best to avoid Gabe's knowing glance as he hauled the saddle off Destiny for the second time.

"Good thing you're hanging out with Josie now. Maybe in a week or so you'll be desensitized enough to have a working brain." Gabe carried the saddle and blanket into the barn.

Jack plopped Destiny's saddle on the hitching post so he wouldn't have to follow Gabe and put up with more ribbing. He had to get a grip. If he continued to wander around in a daze, people would notice, and they might start asking questions.

Questions could lead to assumptions, which could lead to everyone paying more attention to what he and Josie were up to. Jack didn't want anyone to know about this new arrangement for obvious reasons. His family was already watching to see whether he and Josie would make it through the wedding without an incident. If they had any idea that he and Josie were going off into the woods for something besides riding lessons, Jack would never hear the end of it.

JOSIE WAS ALREADY behind the bar serving happy hour drinks when her brother came back from his day hike. When he walked into the bar wearing shorts and a Cubs T-shirt, several of the women there gave him the once-over. Josie sometimes forgot that her brother was a hunk, because to her he was just Alex, her beloved and also pain-in-the-ass big brother.

But with his blond good looks, broad shoulders and lean hips, he could easily be one of the movie stars that vacationed in the Jackson Hole area. Yesterday Josie had answered a couple of questions from customers who wondered if Alex was from Hollywood.

They could tell he wasn't local. Men from Shoshone wouldn't be caught dead in shorts and a T-shirt. Jeans, boots and long-sleeved western shirts were the uniform around here, whether a guy was a true cowboy or only hoped to look like one.

Alex wasn't a poser. He rejected the idea of trying to be something he wasn't, so he stuck with his shorts and T-shirts during the day and only switched to jeans if the nights were chilly. Josie had offered to buy him a cowboy hat while he was here as a souvenir of his visit, but he'd told her that was silly because he'd never wear it. He favored ball caps.

Today's boasted the call letters of the radio station where he worked in Chicago. Josie wondered if he'd received a message from the station. They'd tried her apartment phone earlier but had said they'd also contact him by cell. She suspected they wanted to know when he'd be coming back.

She was a little curious about that herself. He'd been in town almost a week, and although she didn't want to rush him, she didn't want him to put his job in jeopardy, either. Also—she hated to admit this because it sounded selfish—he might cramp her style. She'd have a tougher time carrying on an affair with Jack while Alex was around.

He settled on a bar stool and smiled at her. "How was the riding lesson?"

She'd known that would be his first question, and she'd practiced her answer several times in her head. She shrugged in feigned nonchalance. "It was okay, I guess."

"No issues?"

"Nope." She turned away to fill a glass with his

favorite draft beer, which gave her a chance to compose herself. Lying didn't come easily to her, and Alex had known her all her life. He'd usually been able to see through her whenever she'd tried to fool him.

"That's good."

Josie felt like a bug under a microscope and decided a change of topic was in order. Those gray eyes of his saw way too much. "Did you get your voice mail from the station?"

"Yeah." He sighed and picked up his beer. "My sub isn't working out. The guy has zero sense of humor, and listeners are calling in to complain."

"So they want you to come back."

He nodded and sipped his beer. "That's what they said."

"So, does that—" Josie cut her question short to fill a couple of drink orders. She'd noticed that Alex hadn't seemed too thrilled that the station was begging him to return.

Finally she was able to get back down to his end of the bar. "So if the station wants you back, does that mean you have to leave?"

He glanced at her and grinned. "Wouldn't be trying to get rid of me, would you, sis?"

"No! I love having you here." She ran a damp towel over the bar's wooden surface to clean off some condensation rings. "I just don't want you to lose your job."

He continued to gaze at her with that knowing smile. "And when it comes to you and that cowboy, I'm a fly in the ointment."

"Jack has nothing to do with anything." She polished the bar some more, even though it didn't need it.

"Liar, liar, pants on fire."

Josie groaned and tossed the towel on the counter behind her. "All right. I might be a tiny bit worried that the longer you stay, the more likely you'll get crossways with Jack."

"Could be."

"I promise you that I have everything under control."

"Do you?"

Josie lowered her voice. "Quit looking at me like that, Alex."

He laughed. "How am I looking at you?"

"You know perfectly well. It's the same way you used to look at me when I was sixteen and I'd sneak out of the house to meet Billy Flannigan. You didn't approve of him, either. In fact, I don't think you've liked a single guy I've dated."

"I can't help it if you've dated mostly losers who don't deserve to kiss the hem of your skirt."

"Now that's the pot calling the kettle black. Your choice in women has been abysmal. I can't fathom what you ever saw in Tiffany, or Sue, or—" She stopped herself as she realized she'd been about to rag on his ex. She could make fun of old girlfriends, but this break with Crystal was too new, too painful to be made into a joke.

"You can say it. Or Crystal. All these hikes I've been taking have given me better perspective. Clear mountain air and all that. Crystal was never right for me. I ignored the warning signs and plowed ahead. Mom and Dad didn't think much of her, and I know you didn't, either, although you tried to be nice, which I appreciate."

"You're welcome." From the corner of her eye, she noticed a customer signaling for a drink. "Excuse me a minute. Gotta take care of the folks at the other end. Be right back."

"Take your time."

Josie filled the orders with her usual cheerful customer service, but her mind was on Alex. He was coming to terms with his divorce, yet he didn't seem ready to go back and reclaim his life.

She broached the subject when she returned. "Don't you think you should go back? They can't keep this other guy if listeners are complaining, and with you dragging your heels, they might—"

"Fire me? It's possible." He picked up his beer.

"I thought you liked that job."

"I did." He took a swallow and set the glass back on the cocktail napkin in front of him. "That call from the station was what I needed to make the decision. I'm not going back. I'm moving here."

Josie's mouth opened, but nothing came out.

Alex chuckled. "I can see you're thrilled."

"I am. Of course I am! But what will you do? Where will you work? Where will you live?" Now that last part sounded ungracious. "I mean, you can stay with me for as long as you like. I only thought you'd want a place of your own."

"Don't worry, sis." His gray eyes danced with laughter. "I'm not planning to drop out of society and sponge

off you. It so happens a radio station in Jackson is looking for a DJ. I've already called them and I'm going in
for an interview tomorrow."

"That's wonderful, Alex. It really is." Josie discovered
she meant it, despite the complications Alex might bring
when it came to Jack. "I've missed you horribly since
moving out here. But you know Mom and Dad will have
a fit if you leave Chicago."

"We'll work on them to retire in Wyoming." Alex
looked more excited than she'd seen him since he arrived. "I hate what happened between Crystal and me,
but if it hadn't, I never would have left Chicago. You'd
have to pry Crystal out of there with a crowbar. I had
no idea I'd be so crazy about this area, but I love it."

Josie laughed, happy that he was so happy. "Maybe
you'll have to buy a cowboy hat, yet."

"I doubt it. Unless that's the only way for a guy to
get women around here."

"Judging from my female customers' reactions to you,
a cowboy hat might be overkill. I can see me running
interference so you won't get mobbed once the word's
out that you're available."

Alex polished off his beer. "Feel free to interfere all
you want. And if you don't like somebody, for God's
sake, say so. After this fiasco with Crystal, I'm not sure
I can trust my own instincts."

"Okay."

"But just so you know, I reserve the right to watch
out for your best interests, too. Which brings us back to
this Jack guy. When's your next riding lesson?"

"Um, tomorrow." Josie tried her best to act as if it was no big deal. She didn't think she'd succeeded.

"I figure I should go, just to keep the guy honest."

Inside Josie was screaming *no,* but she struggled to remain calm. "That's silly. I'll be fine."

"I'm not so sure. Two nights ago, he was drunk and disorderly. I think it would be good for me to keep an eye on this character. I could—oh, wait. What time is the lesson?"

"We haven't settled on an exact time. I need to call him." She would definitely call him if she couldn't talk Alex out of this idea.

"I have my interview with the radio station at nine-thirty."

She almost sighed with relief. "We'll probably go at nine."

"I thought you weren't sure about the time?"

"I knew it would be somewhere around then—nine, nine-thirty, ten." She didn't dare mention the lesson had been extended another hour. That would definitely make Alex suspicious.

"All right. I'm probably being paranoid because I got slam-dunked by Crystal." He put some money on the bar and stood.

Josie shoved the money back at him. "Put that away. You don't have a job yet."

"I will." His cocky smile flashed. "I'm that good."

"And so modest." But she knew he was right. If the station needed a DJ, Alex would get the job.

"I'm going upstairs to call Mom and Dad. Any message you want to give them?"

"Tell them I love them and that you moving here was *not* my idea."

"I was planning to blame it all on you."

She laughed. "Brat."

"Pest."

"Come on down afterward and have some dinner."

"Sounds good. And thanks, Josie. You've helped me get my life back."

"My pleasure." Smiling, she watched him leave the bar. Having Alex around on a permanent basis would be fun...except for the small matter of Jack. She needed to keep those two far away from each other.

THE FOLLOWING MORNING, Jack walked down to the barn and announced to Emmett that the lesson with Josie would be two hours instead of one. He'd take his cell phone in case anybody needed him during that time, but he asked Emmett to handle anything that wasn't an emergency.

Jack had chosen Emmett as the person to notify of this two-hour lesson because Emmett wasn't a gossip. If Jack had mentioned it to Sarah or Gabe, or even Nick, it would be the topic of conversation for most of the morning.

But Emmett didn't pass on information unless someone asked him. Jack was counting on the fact that nobody would. After all, people had a wedding to plan. They didn't have time to keep track of him. Or so he hoped.

He expected Emmett to be surprised at the length of time Jack planned to spend on something that wasn't, strictly speaking, ranch business. If Jack hadn't been such a workaholic for the past ten months, Emmett probably wouldn't have batted an eye. As it was, he looked at Jack as if he'd suggested they dedicate the north pasture as a UFO landing field.

"Is there a problem with me being gone from nine to eleven?" Jack asked.

"No, no problem." The foreman rubbed his jaw, a sure sign that he was thinking. "I just didn't expect you to take these riding lessons so seriously."

Jack gave Emmett the standard answer. "I don't want any problems to interfere with the wedding."

"I understand that, but all she'll have to do is walk that horse a bit and then sit on him when he's standing still. It's not like she'll have to run a barrel race."

"It's not only the riding." Jack could see that Emmett, a logical thinker, needed more background. "Gabe and Sarah want to make sure that Josie and I don't have any leftover bad feelings from when we broke up. They figure if I can teach her to ride without us blowing up at each other, then the wedding will go fine, at least as far as Josie and I are concerned."

Emmett nodded. "Looks like you and Josie are getting along, then, if you're stretching out the time."

"We're doing okay."

"It's good to see you acting a little more like yourself."

Jack realized there was no fooling Emmett. The foreman had known Jack practically his whole life. He'd been there when Jack's mother had deserted the family, so he was one of the few people who knew why Jack had no use for the woman who'd given birth to him. Emmett probably understood him better than anyone, which meant he'd figured out what was going on with Josie.

Jack would rather Emmett didn't dwell on that, so he took the offensive. "How's that vegetable garden at the Bunk and Grub? Did you fix that drainage situation for Pam?"

Emmett glanced away and cleared his throat. "I think so. Took a little digging, but she shouldn't have any more problems."

Jack pressed on. "She's crazy about you, Emmett. You know that, right?"

Emmett met his gaze. "Yes, I do. And if she wants an arrangement that gives us both pleasure, then I'm willing. But I'm afraid the woman's after more than that."

Whoa. Jack had never heard Emmett admit that he was sleeping with Pam, but apparently he was. Well, good for them. They deserved some happiness, both of them.

"Did I shock you, Jack?"

"No," Jack lied. He was always shocked to realize that people over fifty had sex.

"Well, I'm a little shocked that a woman like Pam is interested in a man like me. The thing is, she wants to get hitched."

"Married?"

"That's what she said. And I'm not having any of it. I'll be her boy toy, but I'm not about to become the husband of a woman who's worth four or five times what I am. That's a bad deal."

Jack was still back at Emmett's use of the term *boy toy*. He'd never expected those two words to come out of the foreman's mouth, let alone have them referencing Emmett himself. Jack's world was definitely shifting.

"I hear a vehicle coming," Emmett said. "I'll bet that's Josie, and near as I can tell, you're not ready."

"I don't have the horses saddled, if that's what you mean." But Jack was ready in other ways. He'd packed a blanket in his saddlebag and tucked condoms in the pocket of his jeans.

"Then let's get to it," Emmett said. "I wouldn't want you to waste any time."

From the way Emmett said it, Jack was convinced the foreman knew how precious time was to this endeavor. "Thanks," he said. "I appreciate the help." They walked together into the tack room as a car door slammed.

Josie was here. And within the next hour, Jack would make love to her. He shoved that thought aside. If he let himself think about what lay ahead, he'd be shaking so bad he'd never get the horses saddled.

"Women change everything," Emmett said.

Jack reached for a saddle blanket. "Yes, Emmett, they sure as hell do."

8

JOSIE WAS A LITTLE DISCONCERTED to discover Emmett helping Jack saddle the horses for what was supposed to be a secret rendezvous, but the foreman gave no indication that he found anything unusual about this two-hour ride. Josie assumed Jack had mentioned the longer time frame. With his duties at the ranch, he'd have to.

Emmett was definitely an old-school cowboy. His worn clothes and battered hat indicated a man who cared more for function than style, and Josie was sure the red bandanna poking out of Emmett's back pocket was there for practical reasons and not for the jaunty splash of color it gave his appearance.

Josie's clothing choices had been much more deliberate. Underneath her tight jeans she wore her sexiest black lace panties and bra. She would have loved to appear in her red silk blouse, because Jack used to say she looked hot in it, but she didn't dare tip off Alex to the underlying reason for the riding lesson.

So she'd worn a dark blue shirt, and once she was

in the Bronco, she'd unfastened the top three buttons. When she'd seen Emmett with Jack, though, she'd done up the buttons again. She'd also put on her hat, none the worse for having fallen off during her wild ride yesterday. Jack had retrieved it on their way back to the barn.

She had to believe that Jack had kept their plans for this morning to himself, and yet Emmett must be a savvy guy to be the foreman of such a major operation as the Last Chance. Although she considered herself a gutsy woman, Josie wasn't above being intimidated by an authority figure like him.

Finally she pulled Jack aside and spoke in a low voice. "Does Emmett know anything?" she murmured.

Jack's answer was swift and concise. "No."

"Are you sure? Because he has that way of looking at a person that makes you think he knows everything."

"He might suspect, but he doesn't *know.*"

"I suppose it doesn't matter."

"Nope." Jack checked the bridle on his black and white Paint, adjusting the fit with calm assurance.

Watching Jack ready his horse for the ride sent tingles of sensual awareness through her. There was something very sexy about a man who worked with horses. Growing up in the suburbs of Chicago she'd been surrounded by accountants and computer geeks. Nice guys, smart guys, but then she'd come west and encountered the equivalent of knights in shining armor.

Jack epitomized the breed—strong, silent, elemental. She didn't kid herself that she'd have the same reaction if he traded his cowboy duds for a Brooks Brothers suit.

She craved the denim, the leather, the rakish tilt of a hat and the occasional jingle of a spur. Once Jack had shown up in chaps, and she'd almost had an orgasm on the spot.

Emmett gave Destiny a pat on the rump. "He's all set for you, Josie."

"Thanks, Emmett." She reminded herself to walk over to the left side of the tall horse. "If I intend to keep riding, I should learn how to saddle my own horse."

"Not much to it," Emmett said. "Common sense will take you a long way when it comes to horses."

Josie smiled at him. She liked this guy. She wouldn't mind being friends, if the opportunity presented itself. "Common sense takes you a long way when it comes to most things," she said.

"That's a fact. Need help climbing up on that horse?"

"No, thanks. Jack taught me how to do it." Thrusting her left foot into the stirrup, Josie grabbed the saddle horn and swung her right leg over Destiny's back. As she eased down onto the curved saddle, the sun-warmed leather touched her in places that were already sensitized by thoughts of what the morning would bring.

Once aboard, though, she realized that Destiny was still tied to the hitching post and there wasn't much she could do about it from where she sat.

"Let me fetch your reins." Emmett made it sound as if that was how everyone did it—mounted up and then had someone else untie the horse.

Josie knew better, but when the foreman settled the reins around Destiny's neck and knotted them together before handing them to her, she allowed herself to feel like a real horsewoman. "Much obliged," she said, because that was the kind of language she'd heard in western movies and it just sounded right when a person was sitting on a horse.

"Anytime. You look real natural up there." Emmett touched the brim of his hat. "Have a good ride."

"I'm sure I will." Josie focused on the innocent meaning of that statement, because if she thought about the sexual implications, she'd turn redder than the bandanna in the cowboy's hip pocket.

She glanced over to find Jack watching her interaction with Emmett, a bemused smile on his face.

"Ready to go?" he asked.

"Yes." She meant it. She'd been awake since before dawn. Although she'd worried that Alex might assign special meaning to her behavior, she'd indulged in a long shower, taking care to give her legs a close shave.

She'd been tempted to curl her hair and leave it loose around her shoulders, but then her brother really would know she was primping for this supposed riding lesson. Instead, she'd put her hair in its usual braid after washing and drying it.

"Then let's go." Jack wheeled Bandit around and motioned for Josie to go ahead of him. "Want to try a trot again this morning?" he called out.

She wondered if that was for Emmett's benefit, so the foreman would be convinced they were focused on her riding skills. "Sure," she called over her shoulder, and dug her heels into Destiny's flanks.

The jolting began immediately, and her fanny

bounced against the saddle exactly the way it had the day before. So much for hoping she'd magically be able to ride a trot today. She lost one stirrup and was in danger of losing the other one. Without the saddle horn to grip, she would have ended up on the ground.

Jack caught up with her and grabbed Destiny's bridle. "Whoa, son." He slowed the horse to a walk. "Okay, Josie, get your stirrups back and we'll try that again."

"I don't wanna."

"Come on." He flashed a smile in her direction. "Being able to sit a trot is a basic skill."

"But it's embarrassing to have Emmett see me bouncing around like that."

"I don't know if he even stayed around to watch, but I'm hoping he did."

She bristled. "You want to show off my ignorance? That's not very nice, Jack."

"Depends on how you look at it. The more he sees you as a rank beginner, the more he'll understand about these two-hour lessons."

"Oh."

"Now are you willing to trot, just in case Emmett's still watching?"

Josie secured her feet in the stirrups and kicked her heels against Destiny's ribs. "Let's ride!" Sure enough, she was as bad as ever, but Jack had made an excellent point.

Just when she thought her teeth would rattle right out of her head, Jack came alongside again and took hold of the bridle.

"Easy, son." He brought the horse's gait back to a

walk. "We're out of sight of the barn, so you don't have to punish yourself anymore."

"I figured that was the case, but I was too busy holding on to go for the brakes." Now that she wasn't sitting on a pile driver, she was able to appreciate her surroundings. The soft buzz of honeybees mingled with the chirp of birds and the steady clop-clop of their horses' hoofs on the dirt.

Underneath the scents and sounds of nature hummed her constant awareness of Jack, a low note of excitement in the otherwise peaceful landscape. He cut a fine figure on that big black and white horse. Today his shirt was hunter green, which showcased his dark coloring inherited from his mother, who'd been part Shoshone.

They were headed for the trees, and she wondered how far in he'd lead them before calling a halt. She had virtually no control over this enterprise, and she wasn't used to being passive.

"I need to learn to stop my own horse when he's trotting, don't you think?"

"I suppose so." He glanced over at her, his face shadowed by the brim of his black Stetson. "Although Emmett pointed out to me that the wedding won't be a rodeo. If you can ride at a walk and stay on the horse when he's standing still, that should take care of the wedding part."

"So I really don't need to learn to ride very well at all." To her surprise, she was disappointed. Maybe Alex's decision to stay had something to do with it, but she realized Wyoming was her home now. And a Wyoming girl should be comfortable with horses.

She sat up straighter. "You know what, Jack? I want to learn how to ride. I mean, for real."

"You do? But you've lived here for three years without trying. We were together for six months, and you never said a word about riding, even though you knew I practically lived on horseback whenever I wasn't with you."

"I guess it wasn't a priority. Besides, you were busy and I was busy."

His voice was low and intimate. "Face it. We spent most of our time together in bed."

Images rushed into her mind, heating her blood. She met his gaze and tension coiled tight within her. "Which wasn't a bad thing."

"Definitely not a bad thing." His eyes darkened until they were pools of intensity. At last he groaned and turned his head away. "I swear, all you have to do is look at me like that, and I can't think of anything but getting you naked."

"I'm just as bad, Jack," she murmured. "I want you so much right now that I'm liable to start squishing as I ride."

He reined his horse to a halt and grabbed Destiny's bridle. "Hang on."

"What—"

"We'll worry about riding lessons later. Let's move."

As Jack urged Bandit forward, Josie gripped the saddle horn and prepared to be bumped along until they reached the trees, but instead the motion changed to a rolling gait that was not a trot, but not the full-out gallop she'd ridden yesterday.

"What are we doing?" she called out to Jack as he rode along beside her.

"Finding some privacy!" he called back over the sound of the horses' pounding hooves.

"I mean the horses! What is this they're doing?" Without knowing how, she'd adopted Destiny's rhythm and they were moving together so well she couldn't believe it. She couldn't ride, not really, but this was glorious.

"We're cantering! Watch out for branches!" He guided them into the trees.

"I love cantering!" Josie dodged an overhanging pine branch right before Destiny slowed to the dreaded trot again. Not for long, though. Jack brought both horses to a halt.

"Where are we?"

"Doesn't matter. We're out of the open meadow, and that's all I care about." He vaulted from the saddle, his boots making a crunching sound as he came down on a forest floor littered with leaves, pine needles and small branches. He quickly tied Bandit's reins to a tree.

Josie scrambled down, too, her heart racing from the ride and the reason for it. Jack had decided to quit messing around.

Following his example, she tied Destiny's reins to a tree branch. In the time it took her to do that, Jack had taken a blanket from somewhere and spread it on the ground.

"I see you came prepared."

He glanced at her before hanging his hat on his saddle horn. "Guess I liked your suggestion." He closed the distance between them and pulled her close. "You need to ditch this hat, lady. I intend to make hot, sweet love to you, and your hat will get in the way."

Her pulse hammered as he brought her close enough to feel the hard ridge of his penis pressing against the denim of his jeans. "Maybe you could get rid of it for me, cowboy."

"Be glad to." Holding her tight with one arm, he reached for the hat and hung it on Destiny's saddle without even bothering to look at what he was doing.

"This isn't the only time you've made love in the woods with a couple of horses looking on, is it?"

"No, but this is the first time I've wanted it so bad I'm shaking." He lowered his head until his mouth was nearly touching hers. "Have you ever made love in the woods, Josie?"

"Never, Jack." She discovered that she was quivering a bit, too. Anticipation could do that to a girl.

His lips brushed hers. "So you're a sex-in-the-woods virgin?"

Her laughter was breathless from all the wanting crowding her chest. "Guess so."

"Then I'll be gentle."

"God, I hope not." Clutching the back of his head, she pulled him down and kissed him with all the urgency she'd been saving up for the past twenty-four hours.

He seemed to get the message. Continuing to kiss her, he scooped her up and carried her over to the blanket. Then he lowered her feet to the ground slowly as his tongue explored her mouth in a way that left no doubt as to his next move once their clothes were gone.

Breathing hard, he released her with obvious reluctance and started pulling off his boots. She did the same. They undressed with quick efficiency, tossing each item aside. They'd passed the stage of undressing each other slowly and teasingly. After six months as lovers, they knew exactly how to get naked in the shortest amount of time.

Yet even in the flurry of activity, Josie couldn't help stealing a glance at Jack as he shucked his clothes. He'd always had a magnificent body, but apparently he'd done more physical work than usual in the past ten months because now he was solid muscle. And he wasn't kidding about wanting her.

Apparently she'd have to wait before she could enjoy the benefits of that gloriously erect penis. Jack guided her down to the blanket with kisses that started with her mouth and traveled south until at last he caressed her inner thighs with his tongue.

The blanket was soft, the twigs and leaves underneath lumpy, but she didn't care if she lay on a bed of rocks. She trembled with eagerness. Jack had many talents as a lover, but this might be his greatest one. No doubt he knew that, because she'd told him enough times. If he wanted to remind her of what she'd been missing since they parted, he couldn't have chosen a more potent method.

He began, as he always did, with a soft kiss placed exactly on the spot that generated such an incredible response throughout her willing body. She gasped as that leisurely touch of his lips sent jolts of sensation rocketing through her.

"I've missed you," Jack whispered, his breath warm against her dampness. "Missed doing this." He circled her clit with his tongue.

She moaned and curled her fingers into the soft blanket. She'd lost count of the number of nights she'd dreamed of Jack making love to her this way. Now he was here, and she needed…needed…yes, *that*—the stroke of his tongue, the pressure of his fingers, the moist caress of his mouth, the gentle rake of his teeth.

She writhed, she begged…and then she surrendered to a climax that roared through her with the force of a summer storm. Nearly rendered deaf and dumb by the pleasure, she lost track of time, but it seemed only seconds before he thrust deep. She arched upward, inviting him with the tilt of her hips to sink even deeper.

He said her name on a moan of satisfaction as he cupped her bottom in both hands and moved in tight, locking them together. Whenever they joined like this, they seemed to fit so perfectly, to complete each other so well, that she marveled they could exist separately.

Wrapping her arms around him, she waited for her second favorite moment—when he began to move. He nuzzled the curve of her neck as he stayed quietly within her. "I love this," he murmured. "I love being together like this."

"Me, too."

"I've been an idiot."

She smiled. "Yes."

He nipped at her ear. "You were supposed to say *me, too,* like you did last time."

She lifted her hips, cinching them even closer together. "But I haven't been an idiot."

"No." His breath tickled her neck. "Just me."

And then he began to move, and she couldn't talk anymore. The pleasure was too great for her to form words or to think, or to do anything except whimper. She absorbed the steady rhythm and her body responded as it had from the first time they'd made love.

Rising to meet each thrust, she joined him in the dance they'd created from the beginning, the dance they'd perfected during hours spent like this, giving… and receiving. The spring of anticipation coiled within her as it always did when Jack stroked her this way.

Perhaps it was chemistry, or perhaps it was magic. But making love with Jack nourished her in a way nothing ever had. As her orgasm neared, she held on to him, anchoring herself so that she wouldn't fly into a million pieces.

Yet, when the moment came, she did just that. But Jack was there to gather the pieces together and urge her toward another climax. She reached for it at the moment he found his own release. Together they tumbled into the whirlpool, their cries of joy blending with the sounds of the forest.

Josie lay in a daze of happiness, not caring if she ever left this place, or even this position.

"Josie." Jack kissed her nose. "We have a problem."

"That's impossible." She kept her eyes closed and savored the postcoital glow he'd helped create.

"Maybe not a huge problem, but we'll need to get up."

"I don't wanna."

"Well, you'll have to. Destiny's gone."

9

JACK WOULD HAVE LOVED to spend more time on the blanket cuddling with Josie, but Destiny was nowhere in sight. They weren't very far from the barn, and the horse might have worked himself loose and headed back there. Jack wasn't crazy about having Destiny show up without a rider. That could be tough to explain.

Giving Josie a quick kiss, he climbed off the blanket, dealt with the condom, and started putting on his clothes.

"How can he be gone?" Josie followed his lead and grabbed her clothes wherever they'd fallen. "I tied him to a tree branch, just like you did with Bandit."

"I know, but sometimes he takes a notion to get loose and go back home, especially if he knows he's close." Jack hopped on one foot as he pulled on his boot. "He'll break off the branch if he has to. I should have remembered that." Damn straight, he should have. Years ago he'd encouraged that fool stunt because he'd thought it was funny.

"So you think he went back to the barn?"

"Probably headed in that direction." He muttered a few choice words. "Maybe I can catch him before he gets there." Or before Emmett or one of the other hands spotted him.

Josie fastened the snaps on her shirt and tucked it into her jeans. "What should I do?"

"Wait here. If I can, I'll bring him back and we'll ride in later as if nothing happened."

"What if he's already made it to the barn?"

Jack glanced at her. She looked beautiful all mussed up, but any fool would figure out why she was in such a state. "How good are you at making up stories?"

"Not very."

"That's too bad." He untied Bandit and swung into the saddle. "I'll be back as soon as I can. You might want to fold up the blanket and…" He gave her a helpless glance. He wasn't sure what sort of repairs she could make. The flush of satisfaction on her cheeks was a dead giveaway.

"Don't worry. I'll make myself presentable. Good luck, Jack."

"Thanks." He wheeled Bandit and started off the way they'd come, cursing Destiny under his breath. They'd spoiled that horse rotten, he and his brothers, but he was the worst culprit.

He used to love it when Gabe or Nick would take Destiny to go fishing down at the creek and Destiny would quietly work himself loose and walk home if nobody was paying attention. Jack used to give him an apple as a reward for that stunt.

But that was years ago, and Jack had been too focused on Josie, too blasted intent on doing her. Destiny's parlor tricks had been the furthest thing from his mind. But the damned horse could blow their cover.

He urged Bandit into a canter after he broke from the trees. When he had a good sight line, he pulled the horse to a halt and stood in his stirrups to scan the meadow for any sign of a brown and white Paint. Maybe the horse had stopped to graze. Jack knew he was grasping at straws. Once Destiny got the bright idea to go back home, he always made straight for the barn.

When Jack could see no sign of the missing horse, he tried to think of a plausible story to explain what had happened. He could come up with a million reasons why Josie might dismount—problems with the saddle, the stirrups, the bridle, a pebble in her boot, a speck in her eye. But he couldn't think of a single reason why she'd tie Destiny to a tree and then fail to notice that he'd disappeared from the scene. Except for the real one.

Urging Bandit into a fast trot, Jack rode on until the barn was in sight. Sure enough, that cotton-picking horse was standing by the hitching post. Josie's hat was still hooked on the saddle horn, thankfully, and a piece of the branch she'd used to tie Destiny dangled from the reins. More incriminating evidence. Jack let loose with a few choice swear words.

At that moment, Emmett came out of the barn, spotted Destiny, and took a look around. Apparently he noticed Jack and Bandit coming toward him, because he lifted a hand in greeting. Then he turned back to the horse and began untying the branch from Destiny's reins.

Jack's brain was a wasteland as he rode in and dismounted next to them. He hoped something brilliant would come to him. Nothing did.

Emmett glanced up. "Is Josie okay?"

"She's fine." *Mighty fine.*

Emmett nodded. "Figured that was the case because you weren't running Bandit." He removed the stick and straightened to glance at Jack. "So where is she?"

"You mean Josie?"

"Uh-huh." Emmett's expression remained blank, as if they were discussing a topic of no real interest to either of them. "Any chance she's walking in?"

"No, no. I'll…I'll take Destiny back and fetch her." Jack avoided Emmett's gaze. "We had a bit of…that is, she…I mean, I…" Crap. He was making a mess of this.

"Big fight?"

"No!" Jack didn't want anyone drawing that conclusion, either. He hadn't considered someone might assume he and Josie had fought.

Emmett put a hand on his shoulder. "The way I figure it, these are the problems you were sent out there to fix, so go apologize for whatever fool thing you did."

"But I didn't—" Jack caught himself and started over. Maybe this could work to his advantage. "You're right, Emmett. I need to go apologize."

"Glad to hear you say it, son. You have a tendency to be a tad stubborn when people cross you."

Jack started to protest.

"Like your daddy." Emmett squeezed Jack's shoulder. "But being stubborn isn't all bad. At least you stick with whatever you set out to do. Anyway, you'd best get a move on before anybody notices Josie is MIA. Sarah would have a hissy fit."

"Right." Jack grabbed Josie's hat and mounted Bandit. Accepting Destiny's reins from Emmett, he tied them to his saddle horn. "Thanks for keeping this to yourself, Emmett."

"It's what I'd want someone to do for me. Now, git."

Jack took off at a fast trot with Destiny prancing along beside him as if pleased with his little caper. Jack glared at him. "Next time, you mangy piece of crow bait, *I'll* be the one to tie you to a tree, and trust me, there will be no getting loose. We're not playing this game anymore."

As Jack neared the line of trees, he wondered what time it was, and whether Josie would be interested in spreading out that blanket again. But when he arrived at the spot where he'd left her, he realized that wouldn't be happening. She was sitting on a fallen log with none other than his brother Gabe.

Finicky stood nearby munching on a few tufts of grass. Jack noted that the horse was ground-tied and was staying put, as he'd been trained to do, as all the Last Chance horses had been trained to do, with the glaring exception of Destiny.

"Hey, bro." Gabe glanced up when Jack rode into the small clearing. "I was scouting out the wedding location when I spotted Destiny heading for the barn. I decided to follow the trail backward and make sure Josie was okay."

"Thanks." Jack was irritated by Gabe's lack of confidence in his ability to take care of Josie, but there was no point mentioning it now.

He dismounted and dropped the reins. If Bandit stayed put, Destiny would have to do the same. Too bad Jack hadn't thought to hook them together in the first place. If he had, he and Josie might still be naked on that blanket.

Speaking of the blanket, where was it? Josie had been busy, apparently, because she'd smoothed her clothes, rebraided her hair, and done something mysterious with the blanket, thank God. One look at it and Gabe would have known everything. Blankets out in the woods were code for a sexual encounter.

"I was afraid you two had some big fight when I saw Destiny going back riderless," Gabe said. "But Josie tells me you were both searching for one of her contacts and didn't notice when Destiny left." Gabe didn't look entirely convinced.

Contacts? Josie didn't wear contacts. If that wasn't the biggest whopper Jack had ever heard, but he played along. "Yeah, that's what happened, all right."

"Did you find it?" Gabe asked.

Josie said *yes* at the same time Jack said *no.*

"I found it right after you left, Jack." She gave him a glare that distinctly told him to shut the hell up before he ruined her perfectly good cover.

Jack was impressed. For someone who claimed to be bad at making up stories, Josie was doing okay.

"I guess all's well that ends well, then." Gabe stood and walked over to Finicky. "How are the lessons going?"

Jack had sense enough to let Josie answer, which might have been the smartest thing he'd done recently.

"Pretty soon I'll ride well enough to make it through the wedding," she said. "But I've discovered I want to learn how to ride better than that. I'm lucky Jack's willing to teach me, and for free, too. That's real neighborly of him."

Jack thought the neighborly part might be laying it on a bit thick and he shot a warning glance at Josie.

She just smiled.

Gabe, however, still looked suspicious. "I'd better not hear that he's causing you any trouble, Josie. Maybe you lost a contact and maybe you didn't, but Jack can be a stubborn guy, as I'm sure I don't have to tell you."

"No, you don't." She continued to smile.

Jack was getting a little sick of everyone calling him stubborn. He'd agreed to the riding lessons, hadn't he? He'd given up on his original plan to keep those lessons strictly separated from his sexual needs, too. If that wasn't flexible, what was?

Gabe mounted up and gathered his reins in preparation for leaving. It was about time, as far as Jack was concerned.

"I'll mosey on and let you get back to the lesson, then." Gabe touched the brim of his hat in salute to Josie and rode away through the trees.

"Thanks for coming to my rescue!" Josie called after him.

"No problem!"

"Interfering son of a gun," Jack muttered.

"He was just trying to help."

"He was just trying to check up on me and make sure I'm not making your life miserable."

Josie came over and wound her arms around his neck, bringing with her the scent of peach schnapps. "You're not."

"Good to hear." He filled his arms with warm, soft, willing woman. "By the way, what the heck did you do with the blanket?"

"Buried it under a few pine branches, just in case someone came along."

"Quick thinking, because as it turns out, someone did. My nosy brother."

"He's worried about the wedding, Jack." She massaged the back of his neck. "You can't blame him for that. Morgan wants it to go off without a hitch, and yet she also wants me to be a co-maid of honor and you to be a co-best man. Gabe knows that could be problematic."

Jack closed his eyes and savored her touch. "It won't be." He wanted to kiss her, but he also knew they were running out of time, thanks to Destiny's little caper. He sighed. "We didn't have nearly enough time today."

Josie continued to massage the back of his neck. "There's always tomorrow."

He felt the kinks from ten months of grinding responsibility ease a little. He hadn't considered that someone, a certain someone, might make his burdens easier to bear. "I like knowing I'll see you tomorrow."

"Ditto."

He opened his eyes. "Let's go get the blanket."

"We don't have time to—"

"I know that." He gave her a swift, hard kiss and released her. "But I need to put the blanket back in my saddle bag. We can't go forgetting that it's here and let somebody else stumble on it. That would be a red flag, for sure."

"It's over there, behind that big pine." Josie pointed to a spot at the edge of the small clearing.

Jack walked behind the tree and unearthed the blanket from under the pine branches scattered randomly over it. "Good job." He brushed the pine needles off. "And that story about the contacts was great. How did you happen to think of that?"

"One of my girlfriends back in Chicago wore contacts and she was forever losing them. I figured Gabe wouldn't know whether I wore them."

Crossing to Bandit, who stood quietly like the well-trained horse he was, Jack tucked the blanket back in the saddle bag. "I never realized you had such a devious mind."

"I don't, really. But I don't want people to know our business any more than you do."

Jack buckled the saddle bag before glancing over at her. "People like your brother, for instance?"

"For instance, yes."

"I keep meaning to tell you that Sarah said if he's still here the weekend of the wedding, he's definitely invited."

"You still call her Sarah, then."

Jack frowned. "I've always called her Sarah."

"I know, and I wasn't around your family all that much, being a sore point with your dad, but I distinctly remember Sarah wanting you to call her Mom. I thought maybe, after your dad died, that you—"

"She's not my mother. In fact, she's a hell of a lot more honorable than my mother, so I think calling her by her name is actually a step up."

Josie looked at him without saying anything.

"What?"

"Nothing. Never mind. But speaking of Alex, there's something you should probably know. This morning he's interviewing for a job with a radio station in Jackson. He's decided to leave Chicago and move here."

"Oh." Jack wasn't exactly happy about that, but Josie probably was.

"I haven't mentioned this before, but he came out for some R & R after his divorce. He fell in love with the Jackson Hole area."

"That's easy to do." Jack tried to dredge up some enthusiasm for Josie's sake. "Having family here will be nice for you."

"You don't have to be polite about it, Jack. I'm well aware that you can't be overjoyed at the idea. Having Alex living here is a potential problem for you and me, unless…unless you two can become friends."

"Considering the way we started out, that'll be an uphill battle."

"Probably."

Jack gazed around the little clearing where he'd enjoyed amazing sex with Josie. "I'm guessing this project of ours isn't the best way to endear me to your brother."

"No. He wouldn't approve. He's convinced you're a heartbreak waiting to happen."

Jack turned to face her. "I don't plan on hurting you again, Josie."

"I don't plan on letting you." She stood before him straight and strong, her clear gray eyes filled with a self-confidence he hadn't recognized ten months ago. Maybe it hadn't been there ten months ago.

"I believe you," he said. As he gazed at her, he had an unsettling thought. The person in danger of getting hurt might no longer be Josie.

10

"SET 'EM UP, JO!" Alex came into the bar at noon wearing a grin bigger than Josie remembered seeing on her brother in ages. "I got the job."

"Congratulations!" Signaling Tracy to get Alex a beer, Josie came around the bar to give him a bear hug. Maybe the pain of the divorce was fading. "That's awesome!"

"They want me to start right away. I'll see if Mom and Dad would be willing to supervise if I hire somebody to pack up my apartment and ship the stuff out here."

Josie felt a pang of sympathy for their folks. "They'll probably box themselves up and come along."

"I hope they do." Alex was flying high, his beautiful smile flashing. "I want to sell them on this place as a retirement option in a few years. There's that great B and B, the Bunk and Grub. They could stay there while they're here. They'd love it." He glanced over at the bar where Tracy had placed a glass of beer on a cocktail napkin. "Thanks." He lifted the glass. "Here's to being employed."

"I'd drink to that, but I promised Tracy I'd help with the noon crowd." Josie leaned over and kissed her brother on the cheek. "I'm thrilled for you, though."

"I'm really happy about this." Alex took a swallow of his beer. "In fact, I'm going to suggest the 'rents take some vacation time and come out ASAP so they can see why I'm so excited about the place."

Josie tried to focus on the positives of having her family gather round and not the negative. Her parents had hated the way Jack had ended things last fall, so they wouldn't be happy that she'd started seeing him again.

Not wanting to rain on Alex's parade, she put out a mild suggestion. "If you invite them, you might want to suggest they come after Morgan's wedding. I'll want to spend time with them, and as co-maid of honor, I'll be pretty busy between now and the wedding."

"Good point."

"Plus you're invited to the wedding. I found that out this morning."

"Right. Your riding lesson. How did it go?"

"Excellent." She blocked all thoughts of being naked on a blanket with Jack and concentrated on her experience of cantering through the trees. "I've decided I want to get good at this. I like riding."

"No kidding?"

"No kidding."

"So this Jack guy is actually teaching you to ride and

not using the lessons as an excuse to make a move on you?"

Josie hoped her eyes weren't crossed as she struggled to think of a diplomatic answer to that loaded question. "He—" The cell phone clipped to her belt chimed, and she'd never been so happy for an interruption in her life. Then she recognized the ring. It was Jack's.

"Excuse me a minute, Alex." She moved away from the bar.

"Sure." He returned to his beer, and Tracy came over to offer her congratulations.

Josie watched Alex and Tracy as she answered Jack's call. Tracy had a megacrush on Alex, but he hadn't seemed to notice. Josie hadn't thought much about it before because she'd expected Alex to leave. But now he'd be staying, and he was on the rebound from Crystal. Josie wasn't sure how she felt about Tracy, who was a good ten years younger than Alex, lusting after him.

She moved back into her office to answer Jack's call. "Hey."

"Hey, yourself. It occurred to me that your brother might know by now whether or not he got the job he was interviewing for."

"He got the job." She was a little surprised that Jack even remembered about it.

"Then I have a big favor to ask. Would you let me talk to him?"

"About what?" Josie's pulse rate jumped at the very idea of these two guys having another conversation, even over the phone. The last time they'd met was a complete disaster.

"For one thing, I mentioned the interview to Gabe, and he wants to ask Alex to handle the music for the reception. I said I'd do it and find out what he'd charge."

"You're a strange choice as a negotiator if you really want him to say yes. But maybe you don't."

"No, I do. I'm not planning to ask him over the phone. I'm going to see if I can buy him a drink tonight."

Josie closed her eyes. "Look, when I said you two should become friends, I didn't mean you had to become drinking buddies this very night. There's no rush. Maybe after the wedding, when life settles down, the two of you could—"

"No, it needs to be right away. I should have apologized to him sooner than this, but I was guilty of thinking he'd leave and the whole stupid situation between us wouldn't matter. But he's not leaving, and it's past time for me to talk with him."

During their six months together, Jack had never been eager to apologize for anything. Although his father's death had obviously changed his attitude, she hoped it hadn't made him prone to reckless confessions of guilt.

"You're not thinking of telling him about us, are you?" she asked. Visions of a bar fight to end all bar fights flashed through her mind.

"I'm not a complete moron, Josie. I need to get him to tolerate me before he finds out that I'm—"

"Good, but I'm still not sure about this, Jack."

"Give me a little credit, okay? It'll be fine. Is he around?"

She considered pretending Alex was nowhere in sight,

but that would only prolong the agony. She knew Jack, or at least the old Jack, and once he grabbed hold of an idea, nobody could shake it loose. He'd decided to contact Alex, and he'd do it if he had to resort to smoke signals.

"Hang on a sec," she said. "He's in the bar, but you won't be able to hear each other in there. I'll get him to come back to the office."

"Thanks, Josie."

"Don't thank me yet. He might not want to talk to you."

"If you ask him, he will, especially if he's in a good mood because of the job offer. People will do all sorts of things when they're in a good mood. Look at me. I'm calling to talk to your brother, a guy who currently hates my guts."

That made her laugh. "So you're in a good mood?"

"After this morning with you, my whole body is smiling."

"Mine, too."

"Just think how you'll feel tomorrow at this time. I have big plans for you."

Heat surged through her and settled in all her secret places. "Don't say things like that. I've managed to convince Alex that all we do is ride, so if I get too perky, he'll suspect we do more than that."

"That *is* all we do, Josie. First we ride horses, and then we ride each other."

"Stop it, Jack. I mean it. I can't take this phone to Alex if I'm blushing."

"I wish I could be there to see you blush. Did you

know you blush all over? Your cheeks, your neck, your breasts, your tummy, and especially your—"

"Either you cut that out or I'll have to hang up. I'm telling you, my brother has a sixth sense. Don't forget that you want him to tolerate you before he finds out what you've been doing with his sister."

"You're right, but I'd forgotten how much fun it is to tease you. I'll shut up if you'll go get Alex and put him on the phone."

"All right. I'm going now." Josie laid her cell phone on her desk and walked back into the bar, breathing deeply the whole way. She wanted to appear calm and cool.

Maybe Jack was right to jump on this immediately after Alex took the job. If she continued to see Jack, her brother would have ample opportunity to figure out the relationship and he'd be ticked that she hadn't told him the truth. But if Alex learned to get along with Jack, then maybe the revelation that she was involved with him wouldn't be such a big deal!

As she approached the bar, Tracy was laughing at something Alex had said and Alex was looking at Tracy with way more interest than he had a day ago. Oh, boy. He might have recently had his heart broken, but he was fully capable of breaking someone else's.

She tapped him on the shoulder. "Can I see you in my office for a minute?"

Alex turned and gave her a kiss on the cheek. "You betcha. Can I bring my beer? I'm celebrating."

"Of course you can bring your beer." And if he'd bring his spirit of goodwill along, so much the better.

She led the way, and once he was inside, she closed the door and picked up her cell phone. She stuck her thumb over the small mouthpiece. "Jack's on the line. He wants to talk to you."

"Jack? Jack Chance?"

"Yes. I told him about the interview, and he—"

"Sure, I'll talk to him." Alex took the phone. "Hey, Jack? My sister says that she's enjoying the riding lessons, but I just want to reiterate that I'm watching you, buddy. If Josie comes home with a single complaint about your behavior, I'll be at your doorstep with a bucket of cement."

Josie rolled her eyes. So much for these two smoking a peace pipe.

"No, she didn't tell me about the ant hill and the honey." A smile flitted across Alex's face. "You want what?" He looked at Josie and shook his head. "I don't know, Chance. Accepting a drink from you might compromise my principles."

Just as Josie was resigning herself to the call ending in an argument, Alex laughed.

"I would hate to miss that. Oh, what the hell. We'll have a damned drink together, and if that doesn't work out, we can step outside and settle this the manly way. What? No, I don't think dueling is legal anymore. We'll have to do rock, paper, scissors. Something like that. Want to talk to Josie now?"

She stared at him. They were joking with each other?

Alex shrugged and handed her the phone. "What can I say? He made me laugh. It's tough to hate a guy who makes you laugh." Then he opened the office door and walked back out to the bar.

Josie put the phone to her ear. "What did you say to him?"

"That if he meets me at the bar for a drink tonight, I'll demonstrate how I can hang a spoon from the end of my nose."

"You did not."

"I did, too. It worked with you, and he's your brother, so I figured it would work with him."

"Jack, you're insane." But she remembered that the first night he'd started flirting with her at the bar, his opening act had been hanging a spoon from the end of his nose. She'd decided any guy willing to clown around like that in front of a woman he was interested in might be worth getting to know.

And she'd been right. She'd had more fun with Jack than any man she'd ever dated, which was why the abrupt end to their relationship had hit her so hard. She hadn't been able to believe that Jack could change that quickly from a good-time guy to a brooding recluse. Maybe he was emerging from the darkness at last.

"I'm insane about you," he said softly. "I don't want bad blood between your brother and me to get in the way. I created the problem, so now I'll fix it."

"By hanging a spoon off the end of your nose."

"You got a better idea?"

"Nope. And you better believe I'll be here to catch your act. It's been a long time since I've seen you perform that particular trick."

"I was counting on you being there."

"Just so you understand...you have to be careful to treat me like a good friend and nothing more."

Jack sighed. "I know, and it won't be easy, but I'll manage somehow. Just so *you* understand...the whole time I'll be mentally undressing you."

As JACK DROVE INTO TOWN that night, he remembered how often he used to do that, both before he got together with Josie and especially after. But he hadn't done much socializing in the past ten months. Now that he was officially in charge of all ranch operations, that had seemed like a luxury he couldn't afford.

And yet, because Sarah and Gabe had insisted on it, he'd set up the riding lessons with Josie, which took time away from his supervisory role. Amazingly, nothing had gone wrong while he was out of touch. The hands actually seemed to be getting more accomplished in the past couple of days.

Or at least that's what seemed to be happening. Jack wasn't sure he could trust himself to judge anything when he felt so damned good. The ranch could be falling down around him and he might not notice. That was worrisome, because it was that kind of inattention that had prejudiced his father against his relationship with Josie.

Running the ranch had been Jonathan's primary concern for as long as Jack could remember. Emmett had hinted at lapses in Jonathan's perfect record. He'd lost focus after his divorce from Jack's mother, Diane, according to his longtime foreman.

There'd been the brief affair with Nicole O'Leary,

Nick's mother. But from the time Jonathan married Sarah until the day he died, he'd concentrated nearly all his energies on the ranch and the registered Paints it was famous for. He'd seemed to relish every minute of it.

Jack wasn't like that. He'd never really wanted to be in total charge of the ranch operation, despite his father telling him that was how it would be. Jack had resisted the idea from the beginning. He'd even tried to demonstrate that he wasn't right for the job by slacking off, especially once he hooked up with Josie.

Ironically, that behavior had landed him right where he hadn't wanted to be—in charge. But for the past couple of days, now that he was seeing Josie again, the burden hadn't seemed so heavy.

Part of it might be that he'd allowed others on the ranch to assume responsibility while he was off with Josie. So maybe he didn't have to oversee every last detail, after all. And part of it might be Josie herself, quietly offering him her support.

Whatever the reason, he felt more like his old self tonight, which meant he was ready to show Josie's brother that Jack Chance was an okay guy. If it took the spoon-balancing trick, then so be it. And Josie would be there. The prospect of seeing her again was enough to make him run the town's only red light.

Elmer Crookshanks had been behind the campaign to install the light a couple of years ago, and it was conveniently located at the intersection where his gas station happened to be. Jack, along with several others in town, had always suspected Elmer wanted the light in order to force people to stop long enough to notice his station sitting there. Sure enough, Elmer's business had picked up after the light went in.

It stood to reason. No matter when a vehicle came to the intersection, whether there was any traffic going the other way or not, the light turned red. That gave people time to see the station, check their gas gauge and perhaps decide to fill up.

Jack had fallen into the habit of running the light on purpose, just for the hell of it. Elmer would report him to the county, and Jack would have fun arguing the ticket. He was in the mood to create a little chaos tonight.

No one was in the intersection except Jack. Stepping on the gas, he ran the light. The minute he did, he saw a flash, as if someone had taken his picture.

Now *that* was going too far. Hanging a quick left, he pulled into the gas station, climbed out of his truck, and walked into the small building with its permanent odor of gas and oil.

Elmer chewed on a toothpick as he sat behind the battered metal desk that had been part of the station's furniture forever. Nobody knew exactly how old wiry little Elmer was. His hair was gray and his skin weathered, and people had estimated him to be anywhere from forty-five to sixty.

"Gotcha," Elmer said.

"Was that you with the camera, Elmer?"

"I have it set up with a remote here in the office, so if somebody runs a red light, I can take a picture and send it to the sheriff's department. They said they needed concrete evidence."

"For God's sake, this is Shoshone, not New York City!"

Elmer shifted his toothpick to the other side of his mouth. "Gotta obey the law everywhere. You ran a red light, Jack."

"Which brings up another point. How come the light is always red when I hit that intersection?"

Elmer shrugged. "Bad timing."

"I think you've found a way to alter that signal, or maybe you manually operate it, just like the camera, so it turns red whenever someone gets there."

"How would you know? You never come into town anymore."

"That's about to change, and this traffic signal nonsense is about to change, too. I'll give you a few days to fix it so it cycles the way it's supposed to. But the next time I come through here and there's not another soul at the intersection except me, I expect the light to be green."

Elmer chewed his toothpick a little faster. "Maybe it will, and maybe it won't. Can't say for sure." He looked worried, though.

"I can, and it had better be green." Once Jack was outside, he allowed himself to grin. Now *that* was fun. Next stop, the Spirits and Spurs. Jack was back.

11

JOSIE HAD ALWAYS been able to sense when Jack entered a room, so she knew immediately when he came through the front door of Spirits and Spurs. He glanced over at the bar, and she met his gaze. The cocky smile he gave her was like old times. This was the Jack she remembered.

The four-person country band up on the small stage just happened to be playing a Martina McBride song they once liked dancing to, which only added to the feeling of déjà vu. Josie wasn't foolish enough to believe they could recapture the past that easily, but seeing Jack here looking like his old self was a promising start.

Tilting his hat back with his thumb, he maneuvered around the couples on the tiny dance floor and came over to lean on the bar. "Hi, gorgeous."

"Hi, yourself."

"Is your brother here?"

"He's over at the corner table behind you."

Jack hunched his shoulders and talked out of the

corner of his mouth like an old-time gangster. "Thanks for the tip, doll-face. Is he armed?"

Josie laughed. "You're in a rare mood."

He gazed at her, his dark eyes sparkling with good humor. "I ran the light."

"Uh-oh. You know Elmer uses a remote control camera now."

"I didn't know until I ran the light. He says the county needs the evidence. Is that true, or is he just pulling our chain?"

"It's probably true. I'll bet the county got sick of him reporting everybody and then having them argue their cases. You were the most frequent offender as I recall."

"I thought of it as sport! Anyway, that signal is rigged, and if he doesn't fix it, I'm going to prove it's rigged. Plus the camera's got to go. It offends me."

She smiled as she handed him his favorite brew. "We've missed you, Jack."

"Obviously that's true, if nobody else has the cajones to do something about the doggone light. Anyway, you got a spoon I can borrow?"

"You're not really going to do the spoon trick, are you?"

"I'm not only going to do it, I'm going to attach that spoon here and walk over to your brother's table without letting it fall off."

"Here's a spoon, but wait a minute. I still have a couple of drinks to mix, but I want to walk over there with you."

"Okay, then I'll practice." He began rubbing the bowl of the spoon over his nose.

"Dear God. I'm so sorry I left my camera upstairs."

"A still camera could never capture the artistry of this move. You'd need a Hollywood film crew."

"I'll remember to call you the next time we get some Hollywood types in the bar."

"Go mix your drinks." Jack unsnapped his cuffs and rolled back his sleeves. "I have work to do."

Josie somehow managed to put together a gin fizz and a strawberry margarita, although it took her twice as long because she kept glancing down to where Jack was practicing with his spoon, much to the amusement of the others sitting at the bar.

When she'd placed the drinks on a tray for Carolyn, the night waitress, she hurried back to Jack and lifted the hinged part of the bar to join him on the other side. "Let's go."

"What?" He turned to her, his eyes crossed, and the spoon dangling from his nose.

She lost it, laughing so hard her ribs hurt.

"You need to walk ahead and announce me." Jack turned around slowly, and the spoon remained suspended on his nose.

"If I can catch my breath." Gasping helplessly, she started over toward Alex's table.

Alex stared at her as if she'd lost her mind, which she probably had. Jack had that kind of effect on her.

"Presenting Jonathan Chance, Jr., and his famous suspended spoon act," she said. "Don't try this at home." She stepped aside and swept a hand in Jack's direction.

Jack walked slowly forward, and by now half the patrons of the bar were watching his progress and cheering him on.

"I'll be goddamned." Alex began to grin. "You weren't kidding."

"I wouldn't kid about a skill this impressive," Jack said. "I dare you to try it, Keller." Still balancing the spoon, Jack sat down across from Alex. With a flourish he removed it.

Alex stared across the table at Jack. "I'll take that challenge, Chance. Josie, another spoon, if you please."

"I have one!" said someone at a neighboring table. "I always wanted to learn to do that."

Jack glanced around as if assessing the crowd. "Many are called. Few are chosen."

"I can do this." Alex turned the spoon over in his hands. "I seem to remember you have to rub the curve of it over your nose a few times."

"Want some pointers?" Jack asked helpfully.

"No, thanks. I'll figure it out."

By this time the band had caught on and was playing a countrified version of "A Spoonful of Sugar."

Alex's first attempt failed, but the second time he was more successful, keeping the spoon on for several seconds. "Okay," he said. "I'm ready. Anybody got a stopwatch?"

"I've got five bucks says Chance can beat you!" someone shouted.

"I'll put ten on Josie's brother!" called someone else. "He's a Chicago boy, like me!"

Josie stepped back and watched in admiration as Jack and Alex competed in the first annual Spirits and Spurs spoon-dangling contest. The customers gathered around the contestants as beer and laughter flowed freely. It was the liveliest group she'd seen in…well, ten months.

Alex and Jack took plenty of breaks, and drank their fair share of beer. After an hour, both men were laughing so hard they had to call a halt to the contest. But Jack had accomplished his goal. They'd become drinking buddies, and Alex had agreed to be the DJ at Gabe and Morgan's wedding reception.

Alex even went so far as to slap his new best friend on the back and thank him for providing some excellent entertainment. Then Alex came over to Josie and drew her aside. "I get it, now. I understand why you fell for the guy. He's fun to be around, but…I still want you to be careful."

"I will be." Josie glanced over to the table, where Jack was trying to teach a few of the other customers the spoon trick. "I learned a hard lesson last October, and I'm not likely to forget it."

JACK HAD ACHIEVED his stated intention. He and Alex were on speaking terms and Alex had accepted the DJ's job for the wedding reception. Jack had also found a moment to apologize for trying to hit him when they'd first met, and Alex didn't seem to hold a grudge. But Jack knew that he wouldn't necessarily trust him to get involved with his sister.

That meant Jack's other, more private intention was proving tough to accomplish. He wanted a chance to hold Josie before he drove home. Matter of fact, he wanted to do more than hold her. But he didn't have an available spot, and besides, Alex couldn't know about it.

Jack had decided to hang around and see if maybe Alex would go upstairs to bed before closing. But it was as if the guy sensed Jack's plan, and he stuck like glue. Jack had to hand it to him. The guy had stamina.

Alex couldn't dance country worth a lick, and he looked like a greenhorn in his jeans and Bulls T-shirt, but he got out on the floor as if determined to learn the two-step. Plenty of women were willing to teach him. Jack saw a bright future for that boy when it came to the women of Shoshone.

As closing hour drew near, Jack meandered over to the bar where Josie mixed the drinks for last call. "I was hoping your brother would give up and go to bed, but no such luck."

Josie raised her eyebrows. "And why were you hoping that, Jack? Feeling daring?"

"Feeling desperate. I've been watching you all night long, and other than a casual brush of bodies here and there, I haven't had any contact to speak of." He lowered his voice and leaned closer. "I'm used to ending this kind of evening in your bed."

"Not going to happen." She busied herself with the drinks.

"If I outwait your brother, there's always your office."

Her cheeks turned pink. "Nope. I'm not going to take the risk that Alex will decide to come down and check on me." She put three drinks on a tray and went back to mixing.

"But you wish we could get away with it. I can tell because you're blushing."

"It's warm in here." She moved efficiently, squirting mix into glasses from the nozzles attached to containers under the counter.

Jack imagined squirting the mix over her naked body and then licking it off. "With a little imagination, it could be hot in here. All we need is some privacy. How come we never did it on the bar?"

"Because there's no covering for the windows, in case you hadn't noticed. With light from the streetlamps filtering in, someone might have seen us."

"Kinky."

"Jack, give it up. We can't do anything tonight, and that's that."

"I'm not the kind of guy who gives up easily. I'll just hang around a little longer and see what develops."

"You're wasting your time."

"We'll see about that."

She paused to give him a bemused smile. "Gabe's right. You're stubborn as a mule. Apparently I never told you no before."

"Why would you? We had a good thing going on."

"We did, but now that I think about it, I went along with whatever you wanted. I never denied you a single thing."

He leaned closer, breathing her in. "And I like that in a woman."

"I'll bet." She speared an onion and an olive with a plastic toothpick and plopped them into a martini glass. "But you'll come away empty tonight, Jack, so you might as well face defeat and head home to the ranch."

Jack turned back to the dance floor. "Your brother has worn himself out trying to learn the two-step, not to mention the mental exhaustion of going to that interview. I predict he'll sleep like a rock."

"Go home, Jack."

"Not yet, Josie." He knew, even if she didn't, that persistence usually paid off. Everyone might want to label him stubborn, but he considered himself a master of persistence. The only person he'd never been able to outlast was his father, who'd been the grand master.

His mother, from what little he knew of her, hadn't understood the concept at all. She'd given up at the first sign that ranch life would be hard and might require some sacrifices, or so his father had told him. Jack had no respect for that.

The band finished their last number and began packing up their instruments. Customers drifted out the door, and a few came over to thank Jack for the spoon-dangling lessons. That crazy stunt had brought back memories of his father, too. Jonathan Chance had loved to give people something to talk about.

Jack smiled as he remembered the annual prank involving the life-sized plaster horse standing on the porch roof of the feed store. Every fall, Jonathan and Jack would sneak into town with a ladder and a can of blue paint. When they left, the horse's privates would be blue. No one ever caught them, but everyone in town knew the culprits.

Alex came over to the bar. "I've had it." He stuck out his hand. "But I wanted to say thanks for a very interesting evening."

"You inspired me to get back in training." Jack met Alex's gaze as he shook his hand. "I'm thinking of lobbying to make spoon-dangling an Olympic event."

"You draw up the petition and I'll sign it." Alex paused. "So I guess you'll be shoving off now, right?"

"Soon."

Alex glanced over at Josie. "Need any help closing up?"

"I'll be fine. You go on to bed."

"I'll help if she needs it," Jack said.

Alex hesitated. "On second thought, I think I'll stay down here and stack the chairs."

Josie reached across the bar and grabbed his arm. "Seriously, Alex, it's under control."

"You're sure?"

"I'm sure. Don't act like a chaperone. I can take care of myself."

Alex looked back at Jack as if he had doubts. "If you say so. I really am beat. See you later, Jack."

"You bet." Jack raised a hand in farewell. *Yes.* He started moving around the room stacking chairs on top of tables while Josie got out the industrial-sized broom. They'd done this together a hundred times. More than a hundred.

Jack went to fetch the long-handled dustpan. "Feels nice, doing this again."

"Just so you don't expect a reward after we're done." Josie swept the debris into a pile so Jack could load it into the dustpan and dump it in the trash.

"I'll settle for a kiss." Or at least he'd start there.

She put the broom away. "You're pushing it, Jack."

"One kiss. That doesn't seem like too much to ask." He dumped the dustpan and put it in the closet, which happened to be near the main light switch. He killed the lights, figuring semidarkness could hide a multitude of sins, or a multitude of pleasures.

Her voice sounded hollow in the now-empty room. "I know those moves of yours, and I'm not going along with your evil plan."

"It's not evil." His eyes adjusted and he walked over to where she was standing by the bar. "Surely you can spare me one little kiss." He could feel her heat even before he reached her. Her breathing was shallow and quick. She wanted his touch as much as he wanted hers.

"I don't think we're capable of one little kiss, Jack."

"Then two big ones. And then I'll go home." He gathered her into his arms and groaned. "God, you feel good."

"This is such a bad idea." But she cupped the back of his head and pulled him down.

"Yeah, just terrible." He met her halfway and groaned again as he tasted her sweet, sweet mouth. No kiss had ever been so long anticipated or so thoroughly enjoyed. At first he used his tongue only to explore and caress, but primitive urges soon had him thrusting into her mouth and reaching for the snaps on her shirt.

She broke away, gasping. "Jack, we really shouldn't."

"I know. But I'm dying, here."

"Me, too." She caught his hand and drew him away from the bar. "My office. We'll lock the door."

He managed to swallow a shout of triumph. Thank God she needed him as much as he needed her.

The office was even darker than the main room of the bar, and once she closed and locked the door, he couldn't see much of anything. But he could feel, and as soon as he located her, he had no trouble finding the eager mouth she lifted to his, or the buckle to her belt and the metal button and zipper on her jeans.

She helped by toeing off one boot so that he could get her out of half her jeans. That was really all he needed.

"Your chair," he said between frantic kisses. "Let's use that."

Her reply was breathless. "Okay." She helped him search in the darkness for her desk chair. "Here it is." She guided him to it.

As he sat down, he was already unbuckling his belt and unzipping his pants. The armless chair squeaked as he leaned back and fished in his jeans pocket for the condom he'd brought in hopes he'd get to use it. Ripping it open, he shoved the wrapper back in his pocket. He wasn't leaving any evidence behind.

"Now?" Her voice quivered with eagerness.

"Almost." He rolled on the condom and reached for her. "Where are you?"

"Here." She took his hand and placed it between her spread thighs.

He sucked in a breath as he caressed her, sliding his fingers up and in. "You're so wet."

"I've been like this all night."

"If I'd known that…"

"You know it now. And now that you do, could you please do something about it?"

"Be glad to." Cupping her bottom with his free hand, he guided her into position so that she straddled him on the chair. Then he slowly withdrew his fingers so that he could replace them with his cock.

She slid down with a low, soft moan of pleasure. "I thought we couldn't."

"But we can." Cradling her bottom to him, he closed his eyes and murmured his heartfelt thanks for this moment.

"You're welcome." She braced her hands on his shoulders. "This is one kind of riding I don't need lessons for."

"No. As I recall, you're an expert." His heart thudded rapidly in his chest as he waited, because this was Josie's show. She had to make it happen.

"Even experts can use extra practice." As she rose up, she tightened around him.

Oh, yes. He remembered this, and he was about to have the ride of his life.

She began slowly, sliding up and down with those tight muscles that massaged his aching dick and provided the most exquisite torture imaginable. He wanted her to go faster, but he'd be damned if he'd ask for that. She'd pick up the pace when she was ready.

She bounced a little faster, and then…she went for broke, her bottom slapping against his thighs in a piston-like movement that made him grit his teeth against the climax that hovered ever nearer.

He couldn't hold it. He wanted to, but… "I'm going…to…come…" he said, gasping.

"So…am…I…" Breathing hard, she changed the angle, and then…her spasms hit as she let out a long, keening wail through clenched teeth.

He erupted, his hips jerking upward and impaling her even deeper as he trembled in the grip of an orgasm that went right off the Richter scale. Some deeply buried instinct of self-preservation kept him from crying out.

"Oh, Jack." She slumped forward and rested her forehead against his. "That was so foolish. And so wonderful."

"It'll be okay. No one ever has to know."

"We can't keep up this hiding forever. Sooner or later we'll have to go public."

"That's your decision. You have the protective brother."

"And you have the nervous bride and groom."

Jack had to admit Gabe might look upon this development with skepticism. A love affair always had the potential to blow up, especially with the kind of history he had with Josie.

He sighed. "We'd better keep it quiet for now, at least."

"I agree. And I need to get upstairs before Alex gets suspicious."

"Chances are he's out like a light. He won't even hear you come in."

Jack wished to hell he'd been right about that, but when he and Josie finally got themselves back together and opened the office door, someone was sitting in the shadowy room at one of the tables. It could have been a ghost, if Jack believed in ghosts.

He wished to hell he did. He'd rather deal with a ghost than this guy.

"Okay, Chase," Alex said. "We need to talk."

12

JOSIE SHOULD HAVE known better. Actually, she *had* known better, but she'd allowed lust to overcome her good judgment. One thing she was certain about—she wasn't letting Jack shoulder the blame for this.

"I'm the one you need to have a talk with, Alex." She walked over to the table. After the complete absence of light in her office, she found it easy to see in the semi-darkness of the bar. The streetlamps outside the front windows gave the room a soft glow. "Leave Jack out of this."

"Can't." Alex pushed back the chair he'd taken off one of the tables and stood.

He was about the same height as Jack, and Josie knew for a fact he was in great shape from hiking and rock climbing. In a fight, a fight she vowed to prevent, she couldn't predict who would come out ahead.

Jack came to stand beside her, his gaze firmly on Alex. From the tension radiating from him, he obviously expected a fight. "Go upstairs, Josie. Your brother and I will take this outside. Nothing will get damaged."

"Are you crazy? I'm worried about damage to both of you! I could give a flip about the furniture."

Alex shifted his stance. "I'd like nothing better than to punch you out, Chance, but that wouldn't accomplish anything. I meant what I said. I want to talk." He glanced at Josie. "I guess it's up to you whether you stick around or not."

"Damn right it's up to me, and I'm staying." She was relieved that Alex didn't have violence in mind, but she didn't trust either man to keep the conversation cordial if she left them to their own devices.

"All right." Alex grabbed another chair off the table and set it upright. "Have a seat. Chance can get his own chair."

Jack didn't move. "I prefer to stand."

"I see. Then so will I." Alex gestured toward the chair. "Josie?"

"I'll stand, too." The better to move between them quickly if she had to.

"Just as well, I guess," Alex said. "This won't take long. It boils down to one thing, really. I'm sure you didn't drag Josie into that office, so I have to assume she cares for you."

Josie wasn't comfy having her emotional state bandied about. "You don't know that, Alex. It could be simply an overwhelming physical attraction."

"Come on, Josie. You were with this guy for six months last year. When he left you high and dry, you were destroyed."

She winced. "Not destroyed. Upset, maybe."

Alex seemed to realize he shouldn't have revealed that much. "Well, okay, you were upset, a lot more than you would have been if the attraction were only physical. Besides, you're not the type to have meaningless sex."

"Are you absolutely sure about that?" Josie faced her brother.

"Well, yeah. Yeah, I am."

"You know what I think? I think you don't like the idea that your baby sister might want to have meaningless sex, so you assume I'm not the type to do that."

Jack cleared his throat. "He's right, Josie. You're not the type."

She whirled on him. "You, too? Listen to me, *boys*. Girls can be interested in sex for its own sake, just like you manly men."

"I didn't say they couldn't," Alex protested. "I just said it's not like you, and I stand by that. It's not. Especially given your history with Jack."

He was right, and she knew he was right, but damn it, she didn't like having her feelings put on display when she had no idea how Jack viewed their situation.

She crossed her arms protectively over her chest. "Do you have a point with your dissection of my emotional involvement?"

"Yes. Because I think you are emotionally involved, and I want to know where Jack stands on the matter."

Josie wanted to die. Alex was trying to force some confession out of Jack. "You're seriously asking about his intentions toward me?"

"That's what I'm doing."

Most of the time, Josie loved her brother a lot. But right now, she wanted to strangle him. "That's none of your business, Alex. It's old-fashioned, and archaic, and patriarchal, and—"

Jack stepped forward. "I'm not so sure. In fact, if I had a sister, especially if she'd already had a problem with the guy in the past, I'd be asking the same questions."

Josie stared at him. "Whose side are you on?"

"Yours, which is why I'm going to answer your brother's question as honestly as I can. The truth is, I don't know how I feel about our relationship."

Josie's heart twisted. She hadn't wanted Alex to force a declaration of love, but she would have liked something a little bit more encouraging than *I don't know how I feel.*

"That's what I was afraid of," Alex said. "And it's why I've been worried about my sister taking up with you again. You dropped her before, so if you're not particularly invested, why wouldn't you repeat your past performance?"

Jack tensed. "I've already told her I wouldn't hurt her again."

"Which means what, exactly? That you'll let her down easy this time, give her more advance notice that you're checking out of the relationship?"

"That's not what I meant."

"I've asked around, Chance. It's no secret that whenever you have a girlfriend, you're the one who does the leaving. From all reports, you're what the shrinks call commitment-phobic. So what are your plans for Josie?"

"I don't know."

Josie decided enough was enough. "Alex, I appreciate your concern, but I'm a big girl and I can take care of myself." She turned to Jack. "I'll see you tomorrow at nine for our riding lesson."

"Maybe it's not such a good—"

"I'll be there at nine. That was our agreement."

Jack sighed. "Fine. I'll be there."

"I hope you know what you're doing, Josie." Alex focused his full attention on Jack. "I'm going to respect her wishes and butt out, but I swear, if she ends up in tears, you'll hear from me, and I don't give a damn how old-fashioned, archaic and paternalistic that might be."

"Understood." Jack tipped his hat in Josie's direction. "See you in the morning." Then he walked out of the bar without looking back.

"Josie, I sure as hell wish that you'd—"

"Don't say it, Alex. I have a very good idea what the risks are after tonight. If you'll excuse me, I'm going to bed. Feel free to have a nightcap."

"I just might do that."

"Then lock up when you're done." Josie walked out the front door, the same one Jack had used. It was the closest route to the stairway at the side of the building that led to her apartment. She'd always meant to have a stairway built inside that would run from her office up to the second-floor apartment.

If there'd been one, she never would have made love

with Jack in the office tonight, knowing Alex could come down at any time. But the office was a self-contained unit, which was why she and Jack had made love there so many times, including tonight.

Obviously Alex had become suspicious when she hadn't come upstairs right after the bar closed. He'd appointed himself her protector, and after the way she'd sobbed on the phone to him ten months ago, she couldn't really blame him. She couldn't pour out her troubles and then criticize him for interfering in her life. That wasn't fair, and she'd tell him so…tomorrow.

Tonight she needed a hot bath and some time alone to think this through. Alex was right that Jack had shied away from commitment his entire adult life. That went for his romantic relationships and his dedication to the ranch. When his father was killed, he'd been forced to take control of the ranch, but she sensed he wasn't happy about that.

She wasn't about to force him into making a commitment to her. Maybe she'd kidded herself that he was moving in that direction, but Alex's questions, unwelcome though they'd been, had told her a great deal.

As she closed the door to her bathroom and ran water into the tub, she thought about Jack's reaction when Alex had pressed him for answers. He didn't know. She believed he was telling the truth, and that meant she had some decisions to make. They wouldn't be easy.

JACK WASN'T SURE what to expect when Josie showed up the next morning, so he packed for every contingency. Her breezy manner when she climbed out of her Bronco and came over to the hitching post gave him no clues, either. Ten months ago he'd been able to read her moods, but she'd changed.

She wasn't nearly as open as she used to be, and he had himself to blame for that. But she was here, and she wanted to go for a ride. Her brother hadn't convinced her to dump him. That was something, anyway.

She untied Destiny from the hitching post before mounting up. With only two days of lessons, and interrupted lessons at that, she'd picked up a fair amount of information about how to deal with horses. He wasn't surprised. She was quick, which was one of the things that had attracted him.

He patted his saddle bag. "Sarah packed us some homemade brownies, so I brought along bottled water."

"That was nice of her."

"Yeah, it was." He'd dodged Sarah's questions about how the riding was going. She was well aware that he'd gone into town last night. Not much got past his stepmother, but he'd avoided any conversation about his trip.

He'd never been a blabbermouth, so not talking about himself wasn't anything new. Sarah was watching him, though, and he couldn't shake the feeling that he was going through some sort of testing period.

A soft breeze blew across the meadow as they rode through it. Once again, they had a glorious day of blue sky and puffy clouds, sweet-smelling sage and a hawk circling overhead. Yet something was off, and Jack suspected last night's confrontation had something to do with the uneasy feeling between him and Josie.

He thought about suggesting a trot and decided against it. For reasons he'd rather not examine, he wanted to take it easy today. He wanted Josie to be happy with her riding experience and happy with him. He wasn't convinced that she was, even though she acted cheerful enough.

She turned to look at him. "Tell me again why you insist on calling your stepmother by her first name."

He met her steady gaze. "Is that a trick question?"

"Maybe."

"I'm no good at trick questions." He hated them, actually. "Tell me why you want to know."

"Partly clarification. I vaguely remember you said that you couldn't call her Mom because that's what you called the woman who was such a disappointment to you."

"That's what I said and it's still true. But I sense something behind this whole discussion, something that has to do with last night."

"I suppose it does." She looked quite comfortable in the saddle as she gazed at him. "You know what? I think we should talk about this later."

"We can talk about it never, as far as I'm concerned."

She smiled. "Spoken like the Jack I know. Hey, can we canter? I loved the cantering part and I want to do that again."

Relieved that they'd left a touchy subject behind, he pointed to a tall pine on the far right of the meadow.

"That's where we're aiming. There's a trail through the trees there and it leads to a really pretty spot I wanted to show you."

"That's what's so great about being on horseback. You can see out-of-the-way places that you might not otherwise."

"Exactly." He was more pleased than he wanted to admit that she'd taken to riding with such enthusiasm. He loved being out here, and sharing the experience with her was...nice. He wanted to be angry with Alex for upsetting the status quo, but the man had his reasons, and Jack understood that. He had a protective streak, too.

He looked over at Josie. "Ready to go?"

Her gray eyes sparkled with anticipation. "Yep."

"Then dig in your heels and Destiny will get the message." Jack only had to nudge Bandit and make a clucking sound for the big horse to stretch into a canter. Destiny was on the lazy side, but he also liked to keep up with whatever horse was alongside.

Jack took off and glanced over to find Josie right beside him, her cheeks pink and her eyes alight with joy as Destiny broke into a canter. At that moment Jack realized Josie's happiness had become very important to him. He remembered feeling that way ten months ago, but then his father's death had deadened so many emotions, including his feelings for Josie.

Now they were coming back, and it was exactly like the tingling in his hand or his foot when circulation returned after that part of him had fallen asleep. He couldn't decide whether he liked the sensation or not.

In his experience, too much of that tingling sensation could be dangerous.

But here was Josie riding along beside him, full of life and sexier than any woman he'd ever known. Being with her made him forget about his responsibilities for a little while and just be. For that he was grateful.

As they reached the tree line, he called over to her so she'd slow down. If she couldn't do it alone, he was prepared to grab Destiny's bridle and help her, but she'd kept her feet in the stirrups and one hand on the reins. She guided Destiny into a walk with no help from him.

"You're catching on," he said.

"I hope so. There's not much time left."

"We still have almost a week before the wedding."

"Right. Is that the path?" She pointed to a narrow trail through the trees.

"That's it. Head on down that path. I'll be right behind you."

"Then you can coach me. I want to try trotting again."

"Don't torture yourself, Josie. You can work on that another day."

She glanced over her shoulder. "I want to learn it now. I'm inspired after that canter. Just watch me, okay?"

"If you say so." Jack would have preferred a leisurely pace as they approached the clearing he'd chosen for today's rendezvous. Jouncing along on Destiny's back didn't seem like an appropriate prelude to good sex.

But what did he know? Maybe Josie would find it stimulating.

She kicked Destiny into a trot, and at first her sexy bottom slapped the saddle the way it had the past two days.

Jack cringed every time she came down and hoped she wasn't damaging any sensitive parts. "Push your feet into the stirrups and keep your heels down," he said. "Then sink your center of gravity into your seat and grip through your entire leg."

Her heels came down as she tucked her tailbone under her and sat up straight. And then, miracle of miracles, she stopped bouncing. Instead she moved that delicious behind in rhythm with the horse.

Watching her was so damned erotic that Jack wondered if he'd make it to the clearing without closing the distance between them and pulling her off her horse. She moved easily back and forth, back and forth, and it was way too much like sex for his comfort.

"Jack, I'm doing it!"

"Yes, you sure are." She was doing it for him, too. His balls ached something fierce. "Congratulations. You're becoming quite a rider."

"I had no idea this could be so much fun. I'm thinking I need to buy a horse."

"Now that's just plain silly. We have horses galore at the ranch. Destiny's yours to ride whenever you want, and now that you're more comfortable in the saddle, you can try out some of the others."

"Thank you, Jack, but I...I might need my own."

"I can understand that, but at least you could stable your horse at the ranch." Jack liked that idea a lot.

The Last Chance didn't normally stable horses that didn't belong to the ranch, but he was willing to make an exception in Josie's case. Having a horse in the barn would give her a reason to come out often. Going for rides together could become a regular thing.

"We'll see." She guided Destiny into the clearing. "Oh, Jack, this is lovely."

He had to admit she was right. A canopy of pine and oak sheltered an area filled with wildflowers and ferns. A tiny stream ran along the far edge of the clearing before disappearing beneath the undergrowth. Water gurgling over smooth stones made a slurping sound a little bit like two people having sex.

Outdoor sex took him back to his younger days, before he'd had access to indoor recreational opportunities. With Josie's brother in residence, he didn't have a lot of choice now, but the natural setting had turned out great. It suited Josie.

It suited him, too, come to think of it. He'd forgotten how liberating it could be to make love out in the open with a breeze caressing his bare skin. He was eager to get that program started.

Josie dismounted and tied Destiny by separating the reins and looping them around the trunk of a tree. The horse would have to uproot the whole damn tree to get loose today. Jack smiled. Josie obviously didn't want to be interrupted.

Maybe last night had been only a blip on the radar, nothing to worry about. Josie was acting as if nothing was wrong, as if they'd continue the plan of getting together every morning for a riding lesson and great sex. Jack tied Bandit to a tree and took the blanket, the brownies and the bottled water out of his saddle bag.

"You should put the blanket over here, by the stream," Josie said. "The water sounds like—"

"I know. Like sex." Today they had plenty of time and wouldn't have to rush. His body had started to hum in anticipation, and he enjoyed the buildup of tension. This was good. Very good.

Setting the plastic bag of brownies and the water bottles to one side, he shook out the blanket and laid it close to the stream. "How's that?"

"Perfect." Bracing herself against a tree, she pulled off her boots and socks.

He did the same and had to laugh at what they were doing. "We're like two married people getting ready for bed." He said it without thinking, but once the words were out, he wanted them back, especially after he saw her expression. "That was stupid. Forget it."

"But it's true." She walked over to him barefoot. "In some ways it's as if we've known each other forever." She cupped his face in both hands. "But in other ways, we don't know each other at all."

"Ah, Josie." He pulled her close and gazed into her eyes. Something about the way she was looking at him was unsettling, but he was afraid to put a name to it.

Instead he sought to re-create the magic they'd once known. "Let's take your hair down."

Without saying a word, without breaking eye contact,

she reached for her braid and pulled off the tie, letting it fall to the ground.

"Better." As he'd always done, he combed his fingers from her scalp down through her braided hair, loosening the silky blond strands until they hung around her shoulders in soft waves.

He let all that glorious hair sift through his fingers. Taking her hair down was almost more erotic to him than taking off her clothes. But he decided to do that, too, even though they usually undressed themselves.

As he revealed more and more of her fair skin, he paused to touch, to stroke, to kiss. In the beginning, they'd taken this kind of time undressing each other, but then it had seemed silly when they could get out of their things so much faster by themselves.

Maybe it wasn't so silly. Her soft sighs of pleasure as he released her from the restrictions of her clothes stirred him in a way that flinging garments everywhere didn't. When he finished, and she stood naked before him, her hair flowing over and around the pert tilt of her breasts, he took a moment to look…just look.

"My turn." She reached for the top snap of his shirt.

As she moved slowly through the same process, placing kisses on his chest, he closed his eyes and concentrated on her gentle movements. When had the world become such a busy place that he'd abandoned this simple ritual for efficiency?

He loved every second of this, and yet…he couldn't shake the feeling that she was memorizing him as she went. A woman wouldn't do that unless…no, he wouldn't invite trouble. If something was wrong, making love would fix it. It always had in the past.

But for the first time since he'd known Josie, he wasn't sure making love was the answer. Still, it was the only one he had.

13

Josie had always told herself that Jack made love with his whole being, and that proved he was committed to her. But after his answer to Alex's question last night, she wasn't sure that devoting himself completely to love-making was as significant as she'd thought. Maybe he'd done that with all his girlfriends. Perhaps she was no more special than any of the others had been.

There was one way to find out, but she wouldn't think about that now as she lay naked and panting on the blanket while Jack kissed every square inch of her body. She wouldn't think at all, because Jack was by far the best lover she'd ever had the pleasure of sharing a blanket with. Not that her list of partners was very long, but she had a hunch that Jack would head the list for the rest of her life.

He also had the most impressive package of any man she'd known. And she hadn't paid proper attention to it in the past two days. As he rose to his hands and knees and reached for a condom at the edge of the blanket, she flattened her palm against his chest. "Not yet."

His muscles flexed under the pressure of her hand, and his voice was low and seductive. "But I want you."

"Soon." She pushed against his chest, urging him to rise to his knees as she scooted into a sitting position in front of him. "First, I want this." She wrapped her fingers around his rigid cock.

His sharp intake of breath told her he might not mind the delay all that much. His groan when she cupped his balls told her that he might actually be happy about the delay. When she used her tongue to lick the single drop of moisture from the head of his penis and he tunneled his fingers through her hair to clutch the back of her head, she knew that he was in total agreement with the delay.

As she made slow, sweet love to him in this intimate way, she realized why she'd craved touching him like this. It was now, when she had complete control of his reactions, that he became the most vulnerable. Raw needs surfaced as his breathing grew ragged. Each moan was more intense than the last. She wondered if this time he would abandon himself completely. In their six months of lovemaking, he never had.

He didn't today, either. Gripping her head more firmly, he eased away from her. "No more." His voice was hoarse. "I loved it, but no more."

He couldn't let go, not even here, where no one would know but her. And that, she realized, was what had hurt the most when his father died. She'd wanted to hold him and soothe the agony he was enduring. But he hadn't allowed her to be that close. He hadn't allowed himself that comfort.

As he put on the condom and guided her back onto the blanket, she looked into his dark eyes. They were hot with passion, as she knew they would be, but he was back in control. She was the one who would be vulnerable now, the one who would lose control.

And she did, helpless to stop her body from responding to his smooth rhythm, his urgent kisses, his deep, thorough penetrations that brought forth cries of ecstasy from her kiss-swollen lips. Beside her, the stream echoed the liquid sound of his cock sliding in and out, driving her closer and closer to oblivion.

She gazed into his eyes, looking for a connection that went deeper than this bodily one they shared. For a moment she imagined that she saw it—a temporary glimpse of vulnerability and need. But then it was gone, replaced by fierce determination to give her the perfect orgasm.

That single-minded focus soon had her arching off the blanket. He made her come, and then he made her come a second time before he finally gave in to his own climax.

As he shuddered in her arms, she held him tight and wished…but no, there was no point in wishing that Jack would be different. Instead she wished for the strength to do what she must.

JACK HAD GIVEN IT everything he had, but he could tell as he and Josie dressed that all his efforts hadn't fixed whatever was bothering her. He could always try again, but they were a little short on time for that, and besides, he didn't have much confidence a second go-round would make any difference.

Yesterday she'd been glowing as a result of having sex with him, but today she seemed...sad. That was the only word for it, and it sure as hell wasn't the reaction he was looking for.

But he wasn't the kind of guy who relished asking a woman what was wrong. He wasn't sure he wanted to know, anyway. So instead, once they were dressed, he offered her brownies.

"Thanks." She took one out of the bag and stood beside the stream while she ate it. "These are good. Did Sarah make them?"

"I think so." Jack polished off one of the brownies, and Josie was right. It was delicious. Too bad he wasn't in the mood to enjoy it. "Mary Lou does most of the cooking because we feed such a crowd, but every once in a while Sarah likes to get in there and bake something that's just for the family."

"That's nice."

"Yeah, it is. Ready to mount up?"

"No."

Uh-oh. Here it came. He braced himself.

"I want to talk about why you call her Sarah."

He relaxed a little. Maybe this wasn't going to be a Big Discussion, after all. "It's like I said the last time we talked about this. The name *Mom* means something different to me than it does to other people. My actual mom left, so I don't have good memories to associate with the word. Better to use Sarah."

"Logical." She crouched down to rinse her fingers in the stream.

"It's how I feel."

She dried her hands on her jeans and faced him. "Is it? Or is it how you *think?*"

"I don't get what you're saying."

"I believe that explanation is what you think, but I doubt very much it's what you *feel.*"

"You're talking in circles, Josie."

"Let's go at it from another angle, then. I've heard several times that Sarah would love to have you call her Mom. She's wanted that for years."

He tried to figure out what she was going for. "I guess she still doesn't understand my reasons."

"I think she does, Jack, and that's the problem. You're a smart guy, and you've rationalized this beautifully, but the fact is, by refusing to call her *Mom,* you've maintained a distance between the two of you."

"There's no distance." Anger rose in him. "I adore that woman."

"Then why not make her happy? Why not call her what she'd rather be called?"

"Because it would hurt!" He drew in a sharp breath. He hadn't meant to say that. "What I mean is, it—"

"What you mean is that it would hurt," Josie said quietly. "And you are deathly afraid of being hurt."

His body tensed, beginning with his jaw and going all the way down to his toes. "You have no idea what you're talking about."

"Maybe not. But I do know one thing. This wall you've built around yourself so you won't get hurt again the way your mother hurt you, and the way your dad hurt you when he died—that wall is high enough to keep me out, too. Until you're willing to tear down that wall forever, I won't be in your life." She crossed to Destiny and untied him from the tree. "We'd better be getting back."

Panic gripped him. "Josie, what the hell are you saying? What damned wall? We just made love!"

"I always thought that's what we were doing, Jack, which is what kept me hoping that we had a future together. But I think we were just having sex." Turning away, she mounted Destiny in a smooth move worthy of a more accomplished rider.

This conversation couldn't be happening. Everything had been going along so well, except for last night's set-to with Alex. But Josie hadn't referred to last night, so he didn't think that was the problem.

He walked over to Destiny and took hold of the horse's bridle. "Josie, don't do this. Give it time. We've only been back together for a few days."

She gazed down at him. "How much time should I give it, Jack? Six months? Been there, done that. I didn't like the way Alex interrogated you last night, but it made me aware that you really don't know how you feel about me."

So Alex and his damned questions were behind this, after all. Jack hated this kind of confrontation, but he needed to find a way to turn it around. "I was put on the spot last night and couldn't think very well. But you know I like being with you. That should be obvious. We have a great time together."

"I'm sure you like being around your stepmother, too."

"Of course I do. She's a terrific woman."

"And she wants to be your mother, in word as well as deed."

"Damn it!" Jack blew out a breath. "What is so all-fired important about the name I use for my stepmother?"

"When you figure that out, maybe you'll understand why I'm calling it quits." She glanced at his hand, which still clutched Destiny's bridle. "Let me go, Jack."

"This is no good, Josie. We have the wedding coming up in a few days. Everyone expects us to—"

"Don't worry about the wedding. I'll be fine, and so will you. Neither one of us is capable of ruining the big day for Morgan and Gabe."

"Couldn't we just go on as we've been doing? Why are you making such a point of this now?"

She looked into his eyes. "To borrow your words, because it hurts. It hurts a lot, Jack. Now let go of the bridle."

He decided there was no percentage in keeping her here, so he backed away from Destiny. Josie had made up her mind about him and the stupid *wall* she was convinced he'd built around himself. What a crock.

He didn't have a wall around him or he never would have been rolling around on that blanket with her. But nothing he said would sway her at this point. Well, unless he suddenly agreed to start using the word *mom* when referring to Sarah. For the life of him he couldn't figure out what that had to do with anything, and he wasn't about to be railroaded into something that would feel damned awkward, especially after all this time.

Watching Josie ride out of the clearing was a surreal experience. A horrible experience, to be honest. His chest tightened up and he felt short of breath. For a brief moment he wondered if he was having a heart attack, although that was ridiculous. Heart problems didn't run in the family, and he was a healthy thirty-two-year-old.

That left him with the obvious conclusion that he was reacting emotionally to having Josie cut out on him. That was also ridiculous. He'd done fine without her for ten months, and he could do fine without her again.

But if that was true, how come there was this massive ache in his chest? And the top of his head felt as if it were about to come off. He hadn't had a headache in months, not since…the day his dad died. That was the last time he'd felt this bad.

But that had been different. He'd lost his only remaining parent, so of course he'd feel… Jack paused when he realized the phrase he'd just used. *His only remaining parent*. Strictly speaking, that was true, and yet Sarah had been the equivalent of a parent since he was four.

He didn't think of her that way, though. She was just…Sarah. Why Josie was so hung up on that was a real mystery to him. But he and Josie were done now, for sure. Totally finished. She'd left him.

She'd left him. Jack sat on the ground and stared at the spot where she'd disappeared down the trail. *She'd left him.* His chest tightened up again, and the pressure behind his eyes was intense. Maybe he'd just sit here for a while, until it went away.

It would, eventually. He remembered that from the day his father died, and again at the funeral. The pressure would build up until he thought his head would explode, but if he just waited it out, he'd be okay. All he had to do was sit here awhile.

JOSIE LET DESTINY pick his own way along the path while she swiped at her brimming eyes. She'd managed to keep a lid on her emotions until she'd ridden away, but now the tears kept coming. She needed to get them under control before she got back to the barn.

She also needed a story to explain why she was coming back ahead of Jack. Nobody would believe her, though, no matter what she said, unless she told them the truth. She could always go with that. What a novel idea.

But in the process she had to calm their fears about a wedding fiasco in the making. If Sarah happened to be home when she got there, she'd talk with her. That might or might not help, but Sarah had been married to a man very similar to Jack, and had dealt with Jack himself on a regular basis. She might be the only person who *would* understand.

Once Destiny came out of the trees and the open meadow stretched ahead, Josie nudged him in the ribs. Because he was homeward bound, he took off immediately, cantering across the meadow. The wind whipped the tears away and the excitement of riding this powerful animal soothed her aching heart.

Halfway back her hat blew off, but she kept going. Someone would find it, and if not, it was only a hat. A hat was easy to replace. The love of your life, not so much.

Then again, she'd better hope Jack wasn't the love of her life. If so, she was totally screwed. Jack, near as she could tell, was a lost cause. She might have been speaking Chinese back in the clearing for all the effect her words had on him.

At least Alex would be happy about this. He'd probably congratulate her on making the right decision. And she had. She definitely had. But even good decisions could hurt like a son of a bitch.

When she came within sight of the barn, she slowed Destiny, but instead of walking him, she urged him into a trot. Although she still bounced at first, she found the rhythm and rode up to the barn, rocking gently in time with the horse. She was proud of that.

Unfortunately, nobody was around to notice. Dismounting, she tied Destiny to the hitching post. Now she really did have to go up to the house and find someone, so she could report that she'd brought the horse back. If that someone turned out to be Sarah, so much the better.

She was in luck. When she rang the doorbell, Sarah answered. She was dressed in the kind of outfit Josie associated with the older woman—jeans and bright-colored western shirt that contrasted nicely with her medium-length silver bob.

Her hair. Josie realized with horror that hers was still down around her shoulders and had to be a tangled mess by now. Pair that with her red eyes from crying most of the way here, and she probably looked like a pitiful waif.

But there wasn't much she could do about that now except straighten her shoulders and lift her chin. "I wanted to let someone know that I brought Destiny back and he's tied to the hitching post down at the barn. I haven't learned how to unsaddle a horse yet, or I'd have—"

"Come in." Sarah reached out and took Josie's arm as if to make sure her instruction was followed. "What's happened?"

"Everything's fine, Mrs. Chance. Don't worry about the wedding. Nothing will go wrong, I promise."

"Please call me Sarah, and I'm less worried about the wedding at the moment than about you. Did Jack say something? Do something?"

"No. Jack hasn't done anything." Josie stood in the large living room with its beamed ceilings, mammoth rock fireplace, and Native American rugs hanging on the walls. Comfy leather furniture was grouped in front of the fireplace and a wagon-wheel chandelier hung from the ceiling. She'd only been here a couple of times, but she'd always loved this room.

"Come on back to the kitchen. Let me get you some coffee, tea, water, something."

Josie allowed herself to be guided down a hallway to the left. She remembered it led to the kitchen and dining rooms, both the large one where the hands and any guests ate, and the small one for the family. She'd been invited to one family dinner, but Jonathan Chance's disapproval had ruined the meal for her.

"I apologize for the way I look," Josie said. "I wanted to let you know about Destiny, and I totally forgot about my hair." She had no idea how to explain why her hair was in this state, so she didn't try.

"Don't apologize. I feel somewhat responsible for this because Gabe and I are the ones who suggested the riding lessons. I was hoping…well, never mind." She led the way through the large dining room, empty at this hour of the morning. Four round tables that could seat eight were set for lunch.

Which reminded Josie that she couldn't dawdle. Andy and Tracy could open the Spirits and Spurs without her, but she didn't like to be gone without telling them where she was. "I can't stay long," she said as she followed Sarah into the kitchen, where Mary Lou presided over the industrial-sized stove. Josie smelled chicken baking.

"I hope you can stay long enough to tell me what happened." Sarah moved to the counter where a large coffeepot sat. "Mary Lou, you remember Josie Keller from Spirits and Spurs."

"Sure do." Mary Lou turned. "You were also out here for dinner last summer."

"I was, and it was delicious." Josie tried not to think about that ill-fated family dinner where Jack's father had made it plain she wasn't welcome.

"I appreciate that." Mary Lou met her gaze and smiled. "You look as if you could use something to drink."

Josie discarded the idea of asking for whiskey, straight up. "A glass of water would be great."

Sarah gestured to the coffeepot. "We have coffee. We can make tea."

"No, thanks. I really do have to get going."

Sarah brought her a glass of water and pointed to a chair at a small side table. "Sit a minute. Catch your breath."

Josie hadn't realized how shaky she was until she sank onto the straight-backed chair.

"It's plain that you and Jack had a fight."

"Not really." Josie gripped her water glass like a lifeline. "But I've decided that we're just not meant to be."

Sarah raised her eyebrows. "It's really none of my business, but I'd love to know why you think that."

"Don't get me wrong." Josie had to remember this woman loved Jack as a mother loved a son. "Jack's a terrific guy. But he seems to hold something back, if you know what I mean. At least with me, he does."

Sarah's blue eyes softened in sympathy. "He does that with everyone, honey. Even me."

"I know." She caught herself. "I mean, I figured he did."

Sarah traced the grain of the wood in the old oak table. "I was hoping you might break through that barrier he's erected."

"I don't know how." She paused. "So I'm giving up."

"That's too bad."

"But I want you to know it won't affect the wedding.

I promise you that. I'm sure you can count on Jack, too."

"Oh, I'm sure I can." Sarah looked wistful. "But this would have been a great opportunity to…well, never mind."

"I wish it could have worked out." That was the understatement of the year, Josie thought.

"So do I, Josie. So do I."

14

JACK WOULD HAVE LIKED to leave town, even the country, for the next few weeks. But he still had ranch duties, and then there was, of course, the wedding. He and Nick were in charge of the bachelor party on Thursday night prior to the wedding on Saturday.

Jack knew before Nick even proposed it that they'd have to stage it at the Spirits and Spurs. It was the only good venue in town, which was why the bachelorette party had taken place there the night before. In Shoshone, you either had your bash at the Spirits and Spurs or you moved the event out of town. The only person in favor of that was Jack, and he was outvoted.

So here he was, yukking it up with his two brothers, assorted ranch hands, various guys from around town, Josie's brother Alex and two of Morgan's brothers who'd made the trek with their parents in the family's battered and decal-decorated Volkswagen van. The thing had to be twenty years old, maybe more.

At Sarah's suggestion, Morgan's family had parked

the ancient van at the ranch and were staying there over the long wedding weekend. Jack could tell Morgan was a little embarrassed by her latter-day hippie parents, but they seemed like nice enough people. The Jackson Hole area attracted all kinds, so the O'Connellis' tie-dyed outfits, sandals and beads didn't stand out all that much.

For his part, Jack welcomed the confusion of overnight guests and a crowded dinner table. The hustle and bustle of the wedding preparations camouflaged his misery, making it less obvious to all but a select few—Gabe, Nick, Emmett and Sarah. Ever since the morning when Josie had ridden home alone from their rendezvous in the clearing, Jack had worked hard to avoid being set upon by his stepmother, the foreman or either of his brothers.

Thus far he'd been successful, and nobody had been able to corner him for a heart-to-heart about Josie. That's how he wanted to keep it. The plan had worked well until tonight, because he'd had no need to actually see her.

Although thoughts of her had filled his dreams and most of his waking moments, he hadn't been forced to face her in person. Two hours into the bachelor party, he still hadn't dealt directly with her. Tracy had delivered his drinks and he'd kept away from the bar where Josie was working feverishly to fill orders.

Some would say he was a coward, but he maintained that he was doing her a favor. She didn't need him providing an unwanted distraction. Yeah, right. He had a yellow streak a mile wide down his back and he might as well admit it.

He was just beginning to think he might make it through the entire rowdy evening without ever having to talk to her, when he rounded a table to greet a friend he hadn't seen in weeks and there she was, right in front of him. The tray she had carefully balanced on her spread fingers tilted, and Josie lost her balance trying to catch it.

Jack had to choose between catching the tray or the woman, and he caught the woman. For one incredible moment he cradled her in his arms, bracing himself so that she'd fall against him and not tumble to the floor. The tray, however, went down, spraying sticky drinks and littering the floor with broken glass.

Josie swore softly. Then she lifted her gaze to his, and he saw the agony he felt reflected in her eyes. Damn it. He'd been kidding himself that she was okay after they'd broken up.

"I'm sorry," he said.

"It's not your fault." Righting herself, she moved away and called for a mop and bucket.

But it was his fault. Not the dropped tray and the spilled drinks, but the pain in her eyes. He was to blame for that, because he didn't know how to give her what she wanted.

The party continued, but Jack had no heart for it. He helped Josie clean up the mess, and she thanked him without looking at him again. She probably knew she'd let her guard down and wasn't planning a repeat. He wanted to offer comfort but had no idea what to say. They finished mopping and parted without speaking.

After two more interminable hours, the party started breaking up. Jack figured he and Nick were in charge of getting Gabe home in one piece, so Jack went in search of the bridegroom. But he wasn't anywhere to be found.

Jack glanced around, looking for someone sober enough to ask about Gabe. That person turned out to be Alex. Although Jack wasn't crazy about talking with Josie's brother, he didn't have much choice.

"I'm looking for Gabe," he said. "Have you seen him?"

"Yeah, as a matter of fact." Alex pointed toward the front door. "Left about five minutes ago. Said something about going to see his lovely bride."

"Oh." Jack massaged the back of his neck. "Guess he won't be needing a ride home, then. Thanks for the info."

"No problem."

Jack had turned away to go locate Nick and tell him they could leave, when Alex spoke again.

"Josie told me she broke up with you."

Jack glanced over his shoulder at Alex. "That's right. She did."

"I think it's for the best. I couldn't see it working out between you guys. Too much history."

Jack could have done without that unsolicited opinion. He shrugged. "Could be."

"I'm impressed, Chase. It took guts to show up here tonight."

"Nah. Haven't you heard? I'm immune to all that stuff. Nothing gets to me. See you at the wedding on Saturday, Keller." He glanced away, looking for Nick.

As he searched the room, the air moved as if someone had walked up behind him. Nick, probably. "Hey, let's go home, bro." He turned, expecting to see his brother, but no one was there. And yet, he felt a presence. The hairs on the back of his neck rose. "Dad?"

"Hey, Jack!" Nick hailed him from the far corner of the bar. "You about ready?"

"Absolutely!" The strange sensation of someone standing near him disappeared. He ran a hand over his face. Man, the pressure of this wedding must be getting to him. Now he was imagining ghosts.

Moments later, he climbed behind the wheel of his truck as Nick settled into the passenger seat.

Nick held up a six-pack. "I snagged this for us."

"How come?"

"I figured we could use it. Dominique isn't flying in until tomorrow and you just got kicked to the curb by Josie, so—"

"Thanks for reminding me, dickhead."

"You're welcome. The point is, we're both without women tonight, unlike our baby brother. I propose we find a nice quiet place to get wasted."

Jack laughed. "I don't think we can get wasted on three beers apiece."

"Maybe we'll have to be satisfied with mildly happy."

"I could live with that. Where to?"

"I'm thinking we should head out to the Rock."

Jack nodded in agreement. The Rock was their nickname for the sacred Shoshone site located on the ranch. The Shoshone name was long and difficult to pronounce, and the Rock was appropriate because its main feature was a large flat piece of granite streaked with white quartz. The rock was big enough to park a truck on, although no one ever had.

Jack hadn't been out there since their dad died, and sharing a few beers with Nick might be exactly how he should finish out the night. Maybe the Rock would provide some answers to his problems. "Too bad Gabe isn't with us."

"Yeah, but you know how it is. All he thinks about is Morgan."

Yes, Jack knew how that was. All he could think of was Josie. He put the truck in reverse and backed out of the Spirits and Spurs parking lot before pulling onto the two-lane road leading out of town.

As they neared the intersection, Nick let out a whistle of surprise. "I'll be damned."

"What?"

"The light's green. It's never green."

"I'm gonna predict it'll be green a lot more from now on." Jack smiled. "I think Elmer has seen the error of his ways."

"Did you say something to him?"

"He's a petty little tyrant who just needed somebody to challenge him."

Nick grinned. "Way to go." He rolled down the window as they passed the station and took off his hat so he could lean out. "Good decision, Elmer!" Then he left the window down and turned up the radio. "It's about time the Chance boys got back in the game."

Jack knew what he meant. All three of them had been blindsided by losing their dad in the prime of his life. None of them had expected it, least of all Jack. But life went on, and Jonathan Chance would have been the first to say that. He'd want his sons to make their mark on the town. He'd want everyone to know that the Chance boys had been here.

He'd also want them to look forward, not back. Jonathan had always looked to the future, while respecting the legacy of what his father and mother had given him. Jack was beginning to think he'd been too concerned about keeping things the way they were.

He considered that possibility as they drove the quiet country road with the radio blaring, the way they used to when they were teenagers. Soon they reached the turnoff with its two giant poles and crossbeam marking the entrance to the ranch.

Jack swung the truck onto the dirt road and braced himself for the jolts as they bounced their way over the ruts. "Hey, Nick, what would you think of paving this road?"

"Tonight? I think we'd need a lot more beers for that, bro. Plus we'd have to steal a grader and a paver, and some asphalt, and—"

"Not tonight, numb nuts. But soon. Before it snows."

"I think you'd be wise to wait until after the wedding. Hot tar and bridal bouquets don't really mix, if you know what I mean."

Jack blew out a breath. "Yes, *after* the wedding. How many beers did you have at the bar, anyway?"

"One. I was mindful of my duties as the best man."

"Just wondering, because you're in rare form."

"It's been an interesting night." Nick paused. "I felt him there at the bar with us, Jack."

A shiver ran up Jack's spine. "It was just memories. That's the first party we've thrown there since he died, and you were probably remembering his sixtieth birthday bash."

"Well, sure I was, but...you know me. I don't believe in that stuff. Dominique tried to talk me into the idea that there were actually ghosts."

"There aren't. It's pure imagination." Or so Jack told himself.

"I'm not so sure anymore. I don't know if Gabe mentioned it, but Morgan swears she saw a ghost in there after closing time on July Fourth."

"So there you have it." Jack took a rut too fast and had to grip the wheel to keep the truck on the road. "Women love the idea of ghosts, so Dominique and Morgan are going along with Josie's claim that they're around."

"So you didn't sense something, as if Dad was there tonight?"

Jack didn't want to answer that.

"You did, didn't you?"

"It was my imagination." Jack drove past the ranch house looming in the darkness and onto the road that led to the Rock. "Dad loved that bar, so naturally I think about him every time I go in there, especially when there's a crowd and something special happening, like tonight."

"You know what? I've decided to believe that Dad's ghost comes to the bar now and then. It makes me feel... better, somehow."

"Yeah, you always were the sentimental sap of the family, Nick."

"And you always were the hard-ass, Jack."

"And I wear that label proudly." Or at least he had until Josie had accused him of building impenetrable walls around his heart.

They didn't speak again until Jack had parked next to the flat piece of granite that probably had no powers whatsoever. He liked the spot, though, even if he didn't believe much in the local superstition that a person could find clarity by sitting on the rock.

The moon played hide-and-seek with the clouds, and each time it peeked through, it made the streaks of white quartz sparkle. Jack had loved that sparkle effect as a kid, and he still thought it was pretty. Members of the Shoshone tribe didn't visit this site very often anymore, although they had permanent right-of-way to it.

Nick climbed out of the truck and walked over to the rock, six-pack in hand. "Gabe's missing out. He only has two nights left to be single and crazy."

"Yep, he's the first one to fall." Jack sat cross-legged on the granite beside Nick. It always surprised him that the rock retained so much warmth after the sun went down. He popped the top on the beer Nick handed him. "I guess you'll be next."

"Dominique doesn't want to get married until she's

tied up all the loose ends back in Indiana." Nick took a long swallow of his beer. "She still hasn't decided whether to sell her photography studio there or let somebody else run it. She's not having good luck finding the right person."

"But everything's good with you two, right?" Jack hadn't shared a few beers with Nick in way too long.

"It's good. I hate that she's not here with me, but we both knew that being together would take some time and maneuvering."

"I think Dominique's doing the right thing, taking her time. I have to say, I never expected Gabe and Morgan to move this fast. I hope it's not too fast."

"Are you kidding? Have you seen his face when he talks about her? Hell, if Dominique lived here full-time, I'd be agitating to get 'er done, too. Don't worry. They'll be very happy." Nick lifted his beer can. "To Gabe and Morgan."

Jack touched his can to Nick's and polished off the can. "Hand me another beer, Nick. This was a great idea."

"I have those once in a while." He gave Jack another can. "Oh, while we're at it, let's drink to Emmett and Pam."

Jack choked on his beer. "They're getting married?"

"No, but they should. Or just live together. I don't give a crap about the legal part of it, but Emmett's dragging his feet like an idiot."

"He has his pride."

"Pride isn't going to warm his bed at night." Nick

opened his second beer and raised it. "Here's to Emmett figuring that out."

Jack clicked his can against Nick's, but he wasn't thinking about Emmett. Almost two beers into this session and his tongue had loosened up. "Josie told me I need to give up calling Sarah by her first name."

"She wants you to call her Mrs. Chance?"

"No, dummy. You know what she means."

Nick gazed at him, his expression difficult to read in the dim light from the moon and the stars. "Yeah, I know. Josie's right."

"Hell, Nick, how can I start doing that after all these years? It'll be damned awkward."

"It's damned awkward now," Nick said quietly. "If you think she likes hearing *Sarah* when she wants—and deserves—to hear Mom, then you're stupider than I thought."

Jack stared at the shadowy bulk of the Tetons. "I don't know if I can do it." He sat in silence, finishing the beer.

"Want another one?"

"No. I need to think this through."

"Suit yourself." Nick opened a third beer. "Was that Josie's main complaint? That you won't acknowledge Sarah as your mother?"

Jack straightened. "Hey, I acknowledge her! I remember her birthday, and I get her something nice at Christmas, and I order flowers on Mother's Day."

"Yeah, you really dance around Mother's Day. The card always says just *Jack*. Unless I've missed it, you've never once said *Happy Mother's Day* in person or on a card. Face it, Jack, you don't acknowledge her as your mother."

Jack swore softly under his breath. He already knew Josie was hurting because of him. He hated to think that he'd been causing Sarah pain all these years, too.

Nick sighed. "I probably wouldn't have the guts to say this without a couple of beers under my belt, but Josie's the first woman who refuses to take your crap, and that makes her perfect for you. Don't let her get away."

"It's too late, Nick. I already did."

"Bullshit. It's never too late until you're six feet under."

15

JOSIE HAD COUNTED UP the hours that she'd be forced into proximity with Jack so that she could mark them off in her head and be able to see an eventual end to her agony. The rehearsal Friday afternoon, on horseback, was over, and they were already into the rehearsal dinner at the Spirits and Spurs, so she might only have another hour to deal with him tonight. The wedding and reception were hard to figure, but she was hoping for a maximum of five hours for that.

At least the reception would be at the ranch, and not here. She could escape once her maid of honor duties were over. She loved entertaining people, which was the reason she'd wanted this career in the first place, but Jack wasn't just *people*. Jack was…the sexiest, most appealing man she'd ever met, and he was all wrong for her.

The tables in the bar had been arranged in a horseshoe pattern so that all members of the wedding party could see each other.

Morgan and Gabe occupied the two middle chairs at the top, with Nick on one end and Tyler, Morgan's dark-haired sister, between him and Gabe. Josie was at the other end with Jack to her right. She had considered asking Morgan to change the way the best men and maids of honor matched up so that Josie was escorted by Nick and Tyler by Jack.

But that would have alerted Morgan that all was not well. Josie didn't want to do that, so she'd accepted Jack as her escort and pretended that being linked with him for the weekend was no big deal.

Of course it was driving her crazy, especially when she was close enough to feel his body heat, like now. Every available server had been called in for the private party and Tracy had the meal running smoothly. But Josie looked for any excuse to leave the table and check on things in the kitchen and behind the bar.

She couldn't stay away long, however, or her absence would be noted. That meant spending long minutes within touching distance of Jack. During the course of the meal they'd accidentally brushed hands or bumped knees countless times. He was unfailingly polite and insisted on standing whenever she left and helping her into her chair when she returned.

Finally she'd had enough. She leaned toward him and spoke in a low voice. "You don't have to do that."

"Do what?" He glanced over at her. The men had left their hats on the rack near the door in deference to the occasion, so there was no hat brim shadowing the dark intensity of his eyes.

"Help me with my chair all the time. I'll be up and

down a lot to keep tabs on the food and beverage service. It's not your normal social situation."

He held her gaze. "That's true on many levels."

Her stomach turned a few cartwheels. "I'm just saying that—"

"I know what you're saying." His voice wrapped around her, captivating her the way it always did. "You don't want me to pay so much attention to you."

Looking into his eyes she felt caressed, teased, aroused in ways she longed to suppress and couldn't. "Yes. Exactly."

"I wish to God I could help it, Josie." With that, he turned away and said something to Morgan, the bride-to-be, something that made her laugh.

Although she couldn't make out what it was, the timbre of his words stroked every nerve in her body. Despite knowing—*knowing!*—that he was bad for her, she wanted him more than ever. Taking a deep breath and a sip of water, she fought for composure.

She'd just made a trip to the kitchen, so she needed to stay put. The noise level was high and she tried to take satisfaction in that—lots of noise meant everyone was having a great time.

On the left side of the horseshoe, Sarah was deep in conversation with Bianca Spinelli, Morgan's mother. Sarah's silvery bob and western-cut pantsuit contrasted sharply with Bianca's dark, untamed curls and her gaily colored peasant dress, but the two seemed to be getting along like old friends.

Bianca was a hundred percent Italian and proud of her generous curves. She'd kept Wednesday night's bachelorette party humming with her "if you've got it, flaunt it" attitude. She'd taught everyone some sexy dance moves and expected her pupils to show off what they'd learned at the reception on Saturday.

Morgan's redheaded father, Seamus O'Conner, talked with the local minister, Ed Frye, who'd been asked to conduct the ceremony. Seamus was a hundred percent Irish and proud of his gift for blarney, or so his wife said. Neither of them had wanted to give up their treasured last names, and when the children came along, all seven of them, Bianca and Seamus had rejected hyphenation in favor of a hybrid for the kids—O'Connelli.

From talking with Morgan, Josie knew that growing up with these nonconformist parents hadn't been easy. Vagabonds and counterculture idealists, they'd traveled the country with their brood, never staying in one place for more than a few months. All the kids had names that could be male or female to avoid gender stereotyping, but it made for a lot of confusion as Josie tried to keep everybody straight.

Besides Tyler, two of Morgan's brothers had made the trip to Wyoming—Tyler's dark-haired twin, Regan, and Cassidy, a fourteen-year-old carrottop. They sat on the right side of the horseshoe with Alex, who was keeping them entertained, probably with stories about rock stars he'd met as a DJ.

"Your brother's acted pretty damned friendly toward me recently," Jack said.

Josie turned to find him watching her. "He knows you're not a threat to my happiness anymore." If only she believed that. If only she'd held on to her heart when she'd told him goodbye.

His eyes glinted with an unreadable emotion. "I'm that dangerous?"

Yes. Still. She forced calmness into her voice. "Not anymore."

He looked as if he might be about to say something, but a spoon tapping on a glass drew everyone's attention.

Nick stood. "I want to thank everyone for being here tonight, and especially Bianca and Seamus for making the trip with Tyler, Regan and Cassidy. For never riding horses before, you did well at the rehearsal today."

"Except when Tyler rode through the petunias," said Cassidy.

Sarah waved a hand dismissively. "They'll die with the first frost, anyway. Never mind about the flower bed, Tyler."

"My mom's right, Tyler," Nick said. "You stayed on the horse. That's all that's important. So I just wanted to raise a glass and say, good job, everyone."

Glasses clinked. Josie had only Jack to toast with, and not doing so would look petty. She made the gesture, and their fingers brushed. Heat flashed through her.

"To you," Jack said.

Not wanting to seem a coward, she met his gaze. "Thank you for teaching me to ride."

"My pleasure."

Her whole body tingled. Not good.

"The official toasts will happen tomorrow," Nick

said. "I know Josie and Tyler each have one, and Jack assures me he's written his, so I—"

"Jack's written a toast?" Gabe leaned around Morgan to stare at his older brother.

"Don't get all excited, Gabe." Jack tossed his napkin on the table. "I'm leaving all the sappy stuff to Nick."

"That's a relief," his brother said with a grin. "I wouldn't know how to act if you started getting all sentimental on us."

Josie wanted to shout *but he needs to get sentimental!* She controlled the urge. The Chance family dynamics had been in place long before she came on the scene. All his life Jack had gotten away with shutting down his emotions. To expect anything different was a fool's game, and she'd decided to stop being a fool. Now if she could stop loving Jack, she'd be aces.

Seamus O'Conner, Morgan's father, rose to his feet. "I never write my toasts, but I'll want to give one tomorrow."

His wife rolled her eyes. "Now there's a shocker."

"In fact," Seamus continued, "I wouldn't mind having a word or two now."

"Tomorrow would be so much better, Dad," Morgan said. "Tonight we really don't have time for—"

"Sure we do, Morgan." Gabe, who'd had a fair share of wine, smiled at his future father-in-law. "Take it away, Seamus."

Jack tilted his head toward Josie. "Suck up."

"Mmm-hmm." They used to have these private conversations back when they seemed to view the world in the same way.

"Five bucks says Morgan's kicking him under the table."

"No bet. Ten says Bianca's kicking Seamus."

"No bet there, either. How many minutes you give this toast?"

"Fifteen." She wondered if he was aware that he'd slid his arm across the back of her chair.

"Five bucks on Bianca cutting him off at ten."

"You're on." She shouldn't have kept up the exchange and definitely shouldn't have taken the bet. Old habits died hard.

As Seamus began what was obviously a rambling account of Morgan as a little girl, Josie glanced at her watch and settled back in her chair. Jack's fingers curled ever so slightly around her upper arm. She should tell him to move his hand. But the feather touch was so heavenly, and harmless …

Maybe not so harmless. As Seamus droned on, Jack lazily rubbed his fingertips against her arm. She wore a silk blouse, so he wasn't touching her bare skin, but the fabric transmitted that caress in an increasingly erotic way.

Josie stared at her plate, where the food was mostly untouched. She glanced around the room and noticed Alex watching her. Looking away immediately, she tried to pretend that Jack's touch was accidental, that it was something he wasn't even aware of doing.

But she knew better. She knew *him* better. He was trying to get a reaction from her, and he was succeeding beautifully. Her body hummed and her panties grew moist. Visions of their naked bodies flashed with increasing frequency through her mind. Still Seamus talked.

"Jack," she murmured.

"Six minutes and counting." He kept his attention on Seamus. "Mark my words, Bianca's ready to blow."

She took a breath, then another. "What are you doing?"

"Taking advantage of a golden opportunity." He drew lazy circles on her arm.

"Jack, please."

His grip tightened imperceptibly. "Please, what?"

Please don't stop. Please make love to me until all the reasons why we can't be together are burned away. "Please stop."

He did. When he moved his arm and sat back in his chair, she wanted to weep.

"Seamus, for God's sake, wind it up," Bianca said. "We have a big day tomorrow, and we all need to go home and go to bed."

"Then I'll end by raising a glass to this fine company." Seamus lifted the tankard he'd brought along with him for good luck. "And to the happy couple, Morgan and Gabriel. May good luck follow you all your days."

Everyone echoed the sentiment, and once again, Josie was forced to clink glasses with Jack. She tried to regain their light mood. "Ten minutes, on the dot. You win."

A soft smile flashed and was gone. "Depends on how you look at it." Setting down his glass, he pushed back his chair. "You can pay me tomorrow."

She wanted to shake him until his teeth rattled. He'd seriously hoped that his animal magnetism, which he had in spades, would make her forget that he would gladly give his body, but not his heart. He would never know that his plan had almost worked.

JACK DIDN'T MAKE THE DECISION until hours before the wedding. He wasn't even sure why he was doing this, except it felt right and he was going with his gut. Bandit would stay in his stall for the ceremony and Jack would ride the brown and white filly his dad had been transporting the day of his death.

Bertha Mae would be up to it. He'd worked with her during the past week, and when Josie had cut out on him, he'd devoted even more time to the filly. She was a sweetheart and Jack thought it was high time for her to become an official part of the Last Chance. She'd been ostracized long enough.

But he decided the family members needed to know about it.

Gabe was in the barn helping Emmett weave ribbons through the manes and tails of the horses he and Morgan would ride in the ceremony. He barely looked up when Jack announced his plan to ride Bertha Mae. "That's fine," he said.

Emmett did look up and squinted at Jack. "I'm not sure it's the best idea you've ever had."

"Maybe not, but I want to do it, unless somebody's going to have a fit."

"Not me," Gabe said. "But Emmett's right. Ask Nick and Mom before you go doing something like that."

"That was my plan." Jack headed up to the house and met Nick coming out the front door. "Just the man

I want to talk to. How would you feel about me riding Bertha Mae in the ceremony instead of Bandit?"

Nick blinked. "Why?"

"I'm not sure I can explain that. It's just that her presence here has been like a sore spot that won't heal, and so this past week I've been working with her. She's a great horse, and I...I think this is the perfect time for her to become part of things."

Nick tilted his hat back with his thumb. "Anybody else know about this?"

"Gabe said it's fine. Emmett wanted me to check with you and Sarah."

Nick studied him quietly. "It's something you need to do, isn't it?"

"Yeah, I think so. But I'll reconsider if you—"

"No, I'm not going to stand in your way on this. But I have no idea what Mom will say. It might be tough on her. Or maybe not." Nick rubbed his chin. "She's probably thought about that horse plenty, herself. Go ask her. She's in the kitchen with Pam and Mary Lou."

"Thanks." Jack started up the steps to the porch.

"For what it's worth," Nick called after him, "the more I think about it, the better I like the idea."

Jack paused to glance back at Nick, who was smiling. "That's good."

"It's the sort of thing Dad would have done," Nick said, "giving that filly a chance to be useful again instead of shutting her away. The man hated waste."

"I hope Sarah thinks so, too. I'll let you know." Then he turned and went into the cool interior of the house.

The kitchen wasn't cool, though. Pam had not taken

any guests at the Bunk and Grub that weekend so she could pitch in to help Mary Lou with the food for the reception. The event would be held in the meadow, where a company from Jackson had erected a large wooden platform covered by a canopy. The food Mary Lou, Pam and Sarah fixed this morning would be trucked out to the platform by some of the hands once the wedding party rode back in.

The three women bustled from counter to counter, stacking trays of food and carrying them to the walk-in cold storage that Sarah had insisted on having when the kitchen was remodeled. Jack hated to interrupt, but the whole day would be nuts, so better now than later.

"Sarah?"

She turned, a spoon in one hand. "Hi, Jack. Are you hungry? There are some—"

"No, I'm fine, thanks. But could I talk to you for a minute?"

She gave him a puzzled glance and put the spoon back in the bowl of chicken salad she'd been mixing. "Sure."

Jack realized he didn't often ask to speak privately with her. And lately, never. Nick and Gabe both talked with her, but not Jack. No wonder she'd looked at him funny.

"Let's go out on the back porch." Sarah dried her hands on a towel and led the way out the back door of the kitchen to a little porch with two rattan chairs on it. Mary Lou liked to sit there in nice weather when she took a break, and sometimes she and Sarah would have morning coffee out there.

Mary Lou kept a small kitchen garden out here, along with a little flower bed the bees loved. In summer the back porch always smelled terrific between the flowers and the food cooking.

But it had been fall, and too cold to enjoy the porch the last time Jack was out there. Only a couple of weeks after his dad had been killed, he'd been looking for Sarah to ask her about some detail in the ranch ledgers. He'd found her here, crying.

And he'd done a piss-poor job of comforting her, too. He should have crouched down and wrapped her in his arms, but instead he'd stood by her chair and patted her shoulder. She stopped crying pretty quickly, and now he wondered if she'd done that for his sake, knowing he was uncomfortable with her tears.

"Have a seat." His stepmother took the far chair and gestured to the one nearest the door. "Mm, it's nice to sit down for a minute. Thanks for the excuse."

"Maybe we should have hired a caterer."

"Nah." She smiled. "Pam was dying to get in here and help with the food. Gives her an excuse to hang around the ranch and bump into Emmett. Plus I think Mary Lou would have been highly insulted if we'd brought someone else into her kitchen." She gazed at him. "So what's up?"

"I've checked with Nick and Gabe about this, and they seem to think it's okay, but the final decision is up to you."

"Jack, you are not pulling any pranks on Gabe and Morgan. I don't want you painting stuff on his truck or tying things to the bumper, and that's final."

Jack had been so preoccupied with Josie that he'd forgotten that weddings were prime time for that kind of thing. "Okay, no painting and no stuff tied to the bumper." He wondered what else he could reasonably expect to get away with.

"I mean it, Jack." She tried to look stern, but her blue eyes sparkled with laughter. "If that's what you came to ask about, the answer is no."

"That isn't what I wanted to ask you. I wondered if you would have a problem with me riding Bertha Mae in the ceremony today."

The sparkle faded from her eyes and they grew soft, then watery. A single tear escaped, but Sarah whisked it away at once. "Sure. Why not?" She sniffed.

Jack was dismayed. "I'm sorry. Forget it. I'm a complete bonehead. I should have realized that you—"

"No, no. I want you to. I think it's a great idea." She dug in her apron pocket and pulled out a tissue. "Don't mind me." She blew her nose.

"It's not a great idea if it upsets you. This is supposed to be a happy day for you, and I don't want to cause you pain." Josie's words ran through his mind. Josie thought he was causing Sarah pain every time he used her first name instead of calling her Mom. Was he?

She looked at him, her expression resolute. "It *is* a great idea, exactly the way your father would have handled the situation. Make a grand gesture, lance that wound and move on. I've…I've gone down to see her quite a bit, you know."

"Bertha Mae?" Jack was astounded. "You never said anything. I never saw you."

"Oh, I make sure nobody ever sees me. Sometimes I go before dawn, or late at night. I've told her how hard it is for me, knowing that she's alive and Jonathan is dead. She's…she's a good listener." Sarah smiled weakly.

"Maybe so, but she's not going to be in the ceremony. It's too much."

Sarah shook her head. "It's exactly right. I've been wishing we could have some symbol of your father at the wedding. I thought Nick riding your dad's horse Gold Rush would do the trick, but if you show up on Bertha Mae, that's even better…" She drew a shaky breath. "And besides, I think it would do you a world of good."

His chest tightened. "This isn't about me."

"Oh, it is. It's about you, me, Gabe and Nick." She reached over and put her hand on his arm. "Do this, Jack. I'd be grateful."

He took her hand and closed both of his around it. "I don't want to make you cry."

"Crying isn't always a bad thing. Besides, all mothers cry at weddings. Nobody will think anything of it."

16

"YOU MAY KISS the bride."

Easier said than done. Josie sat astride Destiny, holding Morgan's bouquet, while Gabe whisked off his Stetson and tried to maneuver around Morgan's veiled hat and voluminous ivory skirts. They'd practiced this yesterday, but not in full regalia.

Josie decided if she ever got married, which wasn't tops on her agenda right now, she wouldn't tie the knot on horseback. Or if she got married on horseback, she would specify that all the women could wear jeans and not dresses, which required ruffled pantaloons under them so no one in the wedding party flashed the guests while mounting or dismounting. Josie felt like an extra in *Gone with the Wind*.

The men had it much easier. Gabe's ruffled shirt, string tie, black Stetson and cutaway coat didn't hamper him nearly as much as Morgan's dress. Josie had been trying not to notice how sexy Jack looked tricked out in a manner similar to Gabe. He wore ruffles surprisingly well for such a manly man.

He was mounted on a brown and white horse instead of Bandit, which surprised her. But Jack on horseback was an arousing sight, whether he rode his black and white Paint or not. The horse fidgeted a bit, which caused Jack's thighs muscles to flex and his capable hands to tighten on the reins. Not that Josie was paying attention. Not much.

When he spoke in a low voice, she had to look away, because the tone reminded her of the way he talked to her when they were…whoops, better not think of *that*.

Sarah Chance was taking everything in, not missing a bit of the action. Tears rolled unchecked down her face as if she hadn't noticed that she was crying. Her focus shifted from Gabe and Morgan to Jack, and then to Nick.

Bianca was also crying, but she blotted her tears carefully, as if concerned about her makeup. The event couldn't be as poignant for Morgan's mother since she had her husband at her side. Their two sons flanked them, just as Emmett and Pam had taken a position on either side of Sarah. But Sarah's good friends couldn't replace the man she'd loved for almost thirty years.

Morgan finally whipped off her own hat and veil, slung an arm around Gabe's neck, and pulled him in for a big kiss. The mounted wedding party cheered and Dominique, who was the official wedding photographer, took several pictures in quick succession. The commotion caused Jack's horse to toss its head and prance nervously. As he pulled back on the reins, he glanced over at Sarah.

She blew him a kiss and mouthed the words *thank you*. In return, Jack touched two fingers to the brim of his hat in salute. Josie couldn't help wondering what that was all about.

Gabe and Morgan ended their passionate kiss. "That'll do 'er!" Gabe shouted. "Let's ride!"

With that, he and Morgan took off at a brisk trot.

Jack beckoned to Josie, and the two of them met in the middle of the makeshift aisle. He glanced in her direction. "Ready?"

"Yep." Nudging Destiny with her heels, she rode beside him while sitting the trot very well, if she did say so herself.

"Very good."

She stared straight ahead. "Thanks." Despite not looking at him, she was totally aware of his every move. Jack on horseback had become synonymous with their morning trysts, and she might never be able to ride a horse without thinking of making love to him on that soft blanket he'd kept tucked in his saddlebag.

"You look beautiful."

Her pulse leaped. "Thank you." So maybe the dresses weren't such a stupid idea, after all. Prior to getting on the horse, she'd liked the romantic nostalgia of the high-necked blue dress with its tight bodice and full skirt. It wasn't the most comfortable riding outfit in the world, but she did feel feminine and sexy in it. Even if she had no intention of becoming involved with Jack again, she enjoyed knowing he thought she looked good today.

They rode in strained silence while behind them everyone laughed and talked about the ceremony. Josie realized their formality with each other might become cause for concern. She might as well make conversation now and relieve any awkwardness.

So she asked the first thing that came to her mind. "Why aren't you riding Bandit today?"

"It seemed like the time to introduce Bertha Mae."

She glanced at the brown and white Paint. "That's her name?"

"'Fraid so, poor girl. It's the name she arrived with, and nobody's put thought into changing it."

"So she's new?" Josie couldn't understand why Jack would choose a new horse for such a big occasion.

"She's been here a little over ten months."

Something in his tone alerted her to the significance of that. And then she knew. "This is the horse your father was transporting the day he died, isn't it?"

Jack nodded. "I thought riding her today might… well, help in some way."

The uncertainty in his voice made her breath catch. Jack didn't allow himself to be uncertain. "So that's why Sarah blew you a kiss and said thank you."

"Yeah." He sighed. "But I made her cry, and I hate that."

She gazed at him—so tall, so strong, so vulnerable. "I'm sure it wasn't only you riding this horse," she said gently. "Weddings are always emotional."

"Right, which is why I shouldn't have given her something else to cry about."

"Did she know what you had in mind?"

"I asked her and she said it was a great idea, that it would be another way to make Dad part of the day. Still, I wonder if it was a mistake." He paused. "She's a brave lady. That's all I can say."

Josie's throat felt tight. The heart she'd carefully closed and locked against him was opening again. "She's a lucky lady to have three sons who love her."

"We're the lucky ones, Josie."

"Yes. Yes, you are." She might have said more, but the ride was over. They'd arrived at the canopied platforms where tables and chairs were set up and Alex manned a mobile sound system he'd rented in Jackson.

A love song filled the meadow. An hour ago, Josie would have resisted the words and the melody, but that was before she'd discovered that Jack had taken deliberate action to heal the wounds created when his father died. If Jack could take that emotional risk, then maybe the walls he'd built around his heart were cracking.

"Save a dance for me."

She turned to him, expecting to see in his eyes the familiar heat that she found so hard to resist. Instead his gaze was soft, his smile gentle.

Her heart began to pound. Perhaps Jack was willing to take the biggest emotional risk of all. "I think you're supposed to dance with me," she said. "You know, as best man and maid of honor."

"Oh, yeah. Right. I just meant—"

"Don't worry." She returned his smile. "I'll save you a dance." She'd save every dance for him, because once again, she'd begun to hope.

* * *

JACK HAD WRITTEN a toast packed with wisecracks and inside family jokes. Nick had agreed to follow with a toast full of schmaltz, the kind of sentimental schtick he was so good at. But when Jack stood, champagne glass in hand, he looked at the words he'd written and knew they weren't right.

Although Josie sat beside him at the head table, he'd spoken to her very little since they'd ended the ride. He'd avoided talking to her on purpose, because he couldn't make small talk right now. His heart was too full.

He'd never be able to deliver the toast he'd written, either. Crumpling the paper in one hand, he surveyed the assembled guests before turning to Gabe and Morgan.

"Gabe, I owe you an apology. You, too, Morgan, for that matter."

Gabe stared at him. "For what?"

"Thinking you were rushing into this marriage. I didn't get it, didn't understand. I thought you'd lost your minds. But I get it now. You didn't lose your minds, you lost your hearts. I salute you both for having the courage to trust yourselves and each other." He raised his glass.

"Hear, hear!" called Seamus O'Conner. Glasses clinked.

Jack took a sip and remained standing. "There's a man who's not with us today in body, but most definitely in spirit. My father would have loved this party, which was mainly planned and executed by a wonderful woman who's also been the best mother any kid could have, Sarah Chance." Jack met Sarah's gaze as he raised his glass. "Here's to you, Mom."

Her soft gasp of surprise was followed, as he knew it would be, by tears. And it was okay. Setting down his glass, he walked over to her as emotions he'd held in check for years boiled through him, pushing out all the bitterness, all the fear.

Standing, she held out her arms, and he gathered her close. "I love you, Mom," he murmured, his voice thick.

"I love you, too, Jack." She squeezed him so tight he couldn't breathe, but that was okay, too. Then she moved back and smiled up at him through her tears. "And now, I'm *really* ready to party."

"Me, too." Giving her a quick kiss on the cheek, he turned back to the head table.

And there was Josie, his sweet, sexy Josie, with tears running down her face, too. And that was absolutely okay, because he knew they were tears of joy. He wished he could kiss them away, but right now, he had a toast to finish.

He raised his glass again. "To Morgan and Gabe, and a lifetime of love."

Once again, glasses clinked, and Jack made his way back to his seat and sat down.

Josie gazed at him, her eyes still brimming. "That was beautiful."

He wanted to kiss her more than he wanted to breathe, but now was not the time. "No, *you're* beautiful. That was…long overdue."

"Jack, I wish we—"

"I know. Me, too." He reached over and squeezed her hand. "Later."

Nick stood. "I've had to follow Jack all my life, and it's never been tougher to do than right now. Great job, bro."

"I learned everything I know about sappy stuff from you, kid."

The comment got a laugh, which Jack had counted on. Enough of the heavy stuff. Time to lighten up. But he hadn't quite been able to let go of Josie's hand, and he held it through Nick's toast, and through Seamus's endless speech. When Bianca finally put a stop to her husband's rambling, the toasts ended and the dancing began.

Once the bride and groom had their time on the floor and had separated so that Morgan could dance with Seamus and Gabe with Sarah, Jack pushed back his chair. "Our turn."

His arms ached to hold her, and maneuvering around the table so they could access the dance floor seemed to take forever. But at last they made it. When she turned to face him and moved into his embrace, he forgot all about dancing. At last she was in his arms, and he was never letting go.

He gazed into those soft gray eyes. "I've been such a fool, Josie." The words came out without warning. He hadn't planned to say anything until they'd danced for a while, but he couldn't seem to control the emotions surging through him or the urge to tell her everything. "There's no forgiving how I treated you last October, but that's what I'm asking you to do."

The glow in her eyes gave him hope.

He plunged on. "In fact, I'm begging you to forgive me."

"Of course I do."

The tightness that had gripped him since early morning eased, leaving his legs a little rubbery. "Thank God for that. The thing is…" He searched her expression, trying to convince himself that she wouldn't shoot him down, although she still might. What the hell, he had to say it, anyway. "The thing is…I love you."

Her smile trembled. "Good, because I've loved you since last summer."

"Oh, Josie." He framed her face with shaking hands. "I've loved you from that first night we spent together, but I was too stupid—no, too *stubborn*—to admit it."

"Some things take time."

He absorbed the happiness radiating from her. How he'd missed that. "Some things take a lifetime."

"Yes." Her gray eyes sparkled.

"Will you give me a lifetime, Josie?"

Her smile dazzled him. "You know I will."

"I didn't know it before." He brushed her cheeks with his thumbs. "I didn't let myself see the love in your eyes. But I see it now."

"Hey!" Nick called. "You two gonna dance or what?"

Jack ignored his brother as he focused on Josie. "We'll dance in a minute, okay?"

"Okay."

"First there's something I need to do." Right before

he kissed her, he closed his eyes and silently promised to keep his heart open—to Gabe, to Nick, to Sarah, and most of all to Josie, the woman who had claimed it for her own.

Epilogue

HANDLING THE DJ DUTIES at a wedding had a surreal quality for Alex, considering that the last wedding he'd attended had been his own four years ago. Divorce had knocked him for a loop, but he was starting to recover. Still, he wasn't quite so ready to believe in happily-ever-after.

His sister, Josie, believed in it, though, and after hearing Jack's toast, Alex no longer worried that Josie was making a mistake to hook up with the guy. They had an even chance of making a life together, which was all anybody could ask for. Apparently Jack had seen the error of his ways and understood what love was all about. Alex wished he could say the same.

When it came to lust, though, he got it. The minute he'd been introduced to Morgan's sister Tyler at the rehearsal dinner, he'd been hit with a gigantic case of old-fashioned, gotta-have-it lust. He'd spent Friday night dreaming of her bodacious body.

Thanks to his DJ job, he had a perfect view of the dance floor where he could watch her sexy moves. He'd been guilty of bypassing the country tunes at times and deliberately choosing numbers that cried out for swiveling hips and shimmying breasts. Tyler's mother, Bianca, could dance, but Tyler took that inherited sense of rhythm to a whole new level. Alex would love to have some of that action directed his way.

The idea was pure fantasy. Tyler would be leaving Wyoming tomorrow with the rest of her family. Alex knew nothing about her life or whether she had a boyfriend back home, wherever home was. He knew she was twenty-six, because he'd talked with her twin brother, Regan, at the rehearsal dinner.

He hadn't quizzed Regan about his twin because that would have been way too obvious. And stupid. He and Tyler would be occupying the same geographical space for another twelve hours, tops.

In some ways that would be ideal for him, though. Getting it on with Tyler would simply be rebound sex, nothing more. He didn't have the psychic energy for an actual relationship. No telling what her agenda would be, or if she'd even noticed him. He thought she might have. A couple of times he'd caught her giving him the once-over.

In any case, fantasizing about her naked had livened up this gig. He almost hated to see it end, because then he couldn't ogle her on the dance floor anymore. But end it did. Darkness crept over the meadow, the guests began to leave, and he started packing up the gear.

"You did a fantastic job."

He glanced up to discover the object of last night's wet

dream standing before him, her black curls in disarray and her dark, long-lashed eyes shining with pleasure.

"Thanks." He couldn't think of a single other thing to say. This wasn't the sort of situation where he could ask her out for a drink. The only bar was several miles away.

"You picked a lot of my favorite songs."

"That's good to hear." He tried not to stare at her full mouth, the mouth he would not be kissing except in his dreams tonight.

"I was hoping we'd get a chance to talk, but you had to play music and I had to help keep the party going."

"Right." God, she was luscious.

"We're both done, though."

"Uh-huh." His pulse rate jumped. She was going somewhere with this, and wherever she was headed, he'd gladly follow.

She held up a bottle of champagne and two glasses. "Ever had champagne in a hayloft?"

His response stuck in his throat and he had to clear it before answering. "Nope."

"Me, either, but I plan to tonight."

"Sounds…fun." Brilliant, just brilliant.

"Anyway, I'll be up there in about fifteen minutes." She winked at him. "And I have an extra glass."

Alex tried to tell himself he had more sense than to accept that invitation. But in his heart, he knew a hayloft was in his immediate future. Hot damn.

* * * * *

THE SEXY DEVIL & SEDUCING A SEAL
(2-IN-1 ANTHOLOGY)
BY KATE HOFFMANN & JAMIE SOBRATO

The Sexy Devil

Max Morgan. Unrepentantly sexy. Impossible to resist. He's broken countless hearts across the country—including Angela Weatherby's...

Seducing a SEAL

Lieutenant Commander Kylie Thomas has been having inappropriate thoughts about Ensign Drew MacLeod. Can she throw caution to the wind for six feet of blue-eyed perfection?

DANGEROUS CURVES
BY KAREN ANDERS

FBI agent Max Carpenter is assigned to protect irresistible DEA agent Rio Marshall in Hawaii. What Max doesn't know is that Rio has been assigned a task of her own—involving him!

LONG SUMMER NIGHTS
BY KATHLEEN O'REILLY

Journalist Jennifer Dale is on assignment in upstate New York and her wickedly sexy neighbour is none other than a fiercely private award-winning author. This could be a huge scoop...

BAD BLOOD

A POWERFUL
DYNASTY,
WHERE SECRETS
AND SCANDAL
NEVER SLEEP!

VOLUME 1 – 15th April 2011
TORTURED RAKE
by Sarah Morgan

VOLUME 2 – 6th May 2011
SHAMELESS PLAYBOY
by Caitlin Crews

VOLUME 3 – 20th May 2011
RESTLESS BILLIONAIRE
by Abby Green

VOLUME 4 – 3rd June 2011
FEARLESS MAVERICK
by Robyn Grady

8 VOLUMES IN ALL TO COLLECT!

MILLS & BOON

www.millsandboon.co.uk

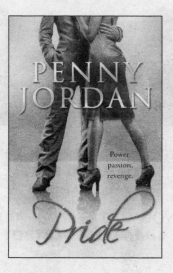

Is the *It* girl losing it?

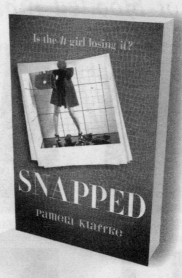

At the helm of must-read *Snap* magazine,
veteran style guru Sara B. has had the joy of
eviscerating the city's fashion victims in her
legendary DOs and DON'Ts photo spread.

But now on the unhip edge of forty, Sara's
being spat out like an old Polaroid picture:
blurry, undeveloped and obsolete.

After launching into a comic series of blow-ups,
Sara realises she's made her living by cutting people
down…and somehow she must make amends.

2 FREE BOOKS
AND A SURPRISE GIFT

We would like to take this opportunity to thank you for reading this Mills & Boon® book by offering you the chance to take TWO more specially selected titles from the Blaze® series absolutely FREE! We're also making this offer to introduce you to the benefits of the Mills & Boon® Book Club™—

- **FREE home delivery**
- **FREE gifts and competitions**
- **FREE monthly Newsletter**
- **Exclusive Mills & Boon Book Club offers**
- **Books available before they're in the shops**

Accepting these FREE books and gift places you under no obligation to buy, you may cancel at any time, even after receiving your free books. Simply complete your details below and return the entire page to the address below. You don't even need a stamp!

YES Please send me 2 free Blaze books and a surprise gift. I understand that unless you hear from me, I will receive 3 superb new books every month, including a 2-in-1 book priced at £5.30 and two single books priced at £3.30 each, postage and packing free. I am under no obligation to purchase any books and may cancel my subscription at any time. The free books and gift will be mine to keep in any case.

Ms/Mrs/Miss/Mr_____ Initials _____

Surname _____
Address _____

_____ Postcode _____

E-mail _____

Send this whole page to: Mills & Boon Book Club, Free Book Offer, FREEPOST NAT 10298, Richmond, TW9 1BR

Offer valid in UK only and is not available to current Mills & Boon Book Club subscribers to this series. Overseas and Eire please write for details. We reserve the right to refuse an application and applicants must be aged 18 years or over. Only one application per household. Terms and prices subject to change without notice. Offer expires 30th June 2011. As a result of this application, you may receive offers from Harlequin (UK) and other carefully selected companies. If you would prefer not to share in this opportunity please write to The Data Manager, PO Box 676, Richmond, TW9 1WU.

Mills & Boon® is a registered trademark owned by Harlequin (UK) Limited.
Blaze® is being used as a registered trademark owned by Harlequin (UK) Limited.
The Mills & Boon® Book Club™ is being used as a trademark.